The Blue Dragon's Geas:

Outcast

Cheryl Matthynssens

DEDICATION

This book is dedicated to my son, Devin.   He taught me that one can live on the outside of the norm, and yet still be truly one with those around him. A valuable lesson for everyone that marches to the beat of their own drum.

.

CONTENTS

ACKNOWLEDGMENTS

A special thanks to Alex Hunt who has walked with me as my editor, and though I have cursed him many times, really forced me to bring my best to the table. I learned a lot in the creation of this book. Also a special note to my cover illustrator, Heather Scoggins, thank you for taking the time to connect the art to the writing.

Chapter One

"Everything has its place...everything but me." Alador sighed to himself as he sat on the cliff's edge looking down at the valley. His village sat back from the side of the river that meandered through broken rock and the contrasting soft meadows of green. From up here, the river looked like a blue snake lazily winding across the landscape. Waves of heat muddled the view slightly as the sun beat down upon the valley floor. The hills that rolled around the edges of the valley looked like one could stroke their soft, fuzzy surface. It was an illusion, of course, as most of the vegetation was rough scrub bush. The mountains and highest hill tops in the distance still held caps of winter snow. The smell of sagebrush, dust, and early spring flowers drifted on the air. It was a perfect blend below Alador; but as he sat up, apart from it now, he realized that he didn't really fit in. It had been that way since he was a small one, yet today it seemed so much more pointed as he looked down at the broken beauty sprawling off into the distance.

He ran a hand through his thick, close cropped hair. It, like the hair of his Daezun kin, was a mundane shade of brown that was almost drab. Unlike his kin, however, his eyes sparkled with silver that looked as if it had spilled from the stars. He was also taller and leaner than his kin, thanks to his Lerdenian father, whose blood had made him an outcast in the Daezun village below. The mixed heritage gave him a somewhat fairer shade of skin, without the ruddy flushed appearance that his brothers had, and made his features more defined.

Alador reached into his canvas pocket and pulled out the small bloodstone he'd found that morning. He stroked its slick, glistening sides and stared at the far off river. Bloodstones were the only way he could help support his mother. As an outcast, thanks to his mixed heritage, Alador hadn't been chosen as an apprentice to any village trade. He couldn't even manage in the family forge, despite the efforts his brother Dorien went through to teach him. Alador was forever ruining the simplest of projects, but perhaps it had more to do with his lack of interest than a lack of ability. His main job when at home was to keep the fires in the forge burning and to work the bellows.

Alador gazed down at the little bloodstone. What he wanted was to follow in his father's footsteps. His father was a traveling enchanter. He'd tested Alador every turn before the mating circle, but Alador had yet to show any ability to feel the power in the stones. He couldn't produce the smallest spark to even a ring-sized piece. It was soon to be that time again. Two more turns and he would be considered a full adult with all the rights of other village males. He would have already begged his father to take him away despite the failed tests if not for his best friend, Mesiande.

As if she'd heard his thoughts, her voice washed over him: "Alador, quit the wool gathering, time to get back to it," she called. The cheerful tones of her voice were musical despite their jarring interruption of his musings. One of two Alador could call friend, Mesiande came from a family of miners and had shown him how to find the stones. She was also the only reason he wanted to stay in the valley.

Alador looked back up at the sun. It had moved beyond the high mark. Light would fade fast once it nestled behind the great hill opposite of where they were working today, so he gathered up his things and shoved them back into his pack. He rolled up to his feet and then, with purpose, cast a pebble out, breaking the stillness as it clattered its way down the hillside below him. He picked up both bag and pick and turned to head down to where Mesiande waited. She was a beautiful middlin, he thought, with long hair braided tightly to stay out of her face during her work. Many mining women kept theirs short; Alador was glad she had chosen to keep its length. Her eyes sparkled with a genuine joy of life.

"Always daydreaming. One day, you'll fall off, being so deep in thought," she teased as Alador approached. Her face was covered in dust, and a few stray hairs bristled from her braid.

"Well, would save you the bother of always having to seek me out," Alador quipped back with a crooked grin. He winked as Mesiande shook her head at his remark. "Come now, you know you wouldn't miss that." They had an easy friendship that Alador loved; her smile always lifted his spirits. It was as if she was a balm that could mend any heartache.

"I wouldn't miss losing daylight and a possible find," she pointed out, hands on her hips. Her face took on a firm, scolding expression.

Her remark brought a tiny bit of guilt, and he lost his smile. "Sorry, Mesi. I'll watch the light better tomorrow." He glanced quickly over as they wandered down to the small ledge the team had been working. Seeing that Mesiande's frown didn't last long, he smiled again. "I'll make it up to you." He offered her the small bit of stone he'd worked free earlier that day.

"I can't take that, not when I know that this is how you earn your keep, Alador." She shook her head and stopped to look at him. "Just remember that it's how I make mine as well."

Alador nodded and led the way down. He pocketed the crystal and they both skirted the pile of dragon bones that had been slowly growing throughout the day. Bloodstones were only found beneath the body of a long dead dragon. Some said that the magic of the dragon leeched into the ground, and that is what formed the stones; others said it was their actual blood that brought about the powerful crystals. Whatever caused it, two things were true: one, the stones were empowered with magic; and two, those who used magic for healing, weather calling, and even illusions paid well for the stones' gifts. There were, of course, also rumors that they could be used for dark arts. Such magics, however, were forbidden by both the Lerdenian and Daezun kingdoms.

There were other lands across the sea said to allow such arts.

Alador returned back to where he'd found a leading wing bone. He had worked a large portion of the bone free already, and now carefully worked the dirt beneath it, looking for its treasure. It had been here that he'd found the small crystal; in fact, the team had been finding small jewelry-sized pieces all day. His trowel hit something with the familiar sound of metal to glass, and he looked about. Everyone was busy. He had already learned that he'd best keep his bloodstones hidden if they were bigger than a small bird's egg. More than once he had been forced to trade for a smaller piece, and he had always given in for fear of being denied to come along. It hadn't taken him long to figure out that it was better to give up one large piece willingly than to be searched for all the pieces that he had. It was just one more way he stood on the outside looking in at a kinship that barely tolerated him. To their credit, the other members of the expedition always ensured his trip was worth the effort even if they had 'traded' his larger stones into their own pockets.

He carefully worked the trowel around the stone. His eyes widened – this was the biggest piece he'd ever seen, easily the size of a melon. There was no way Alador would be able to hide it. He looked around at the others who were still digging steadily. Certainly a piece this large would cause such uproar that they couldn't hide the fact that Alador was the one who'd pulled it from the ground. He reached over casually and took a drink of water from the canister within his bag. Making what would appear to be an attempt to set the bag closer to him in the shade, he returned to the hole. Perhaps he could slip it into his rock bag if he timed it right. He began to work the piece free, but it was stuck as if glued to the stone beneath it. Fearing that the trowel would damage it, Alador reached into the hole to work it free. His gloved hands slid off the slick stone, and it barely budged. He pulled off his gloves to get a better grip and carefully placed his hands on either side. He tugged hard, but it still wouldn't move. He placed his feet against the hill to give himself some leverage. Just as he felt it begin to come free, hot fire shot through his hands, which clutched the stone tightly despite the pain. Screaming, Alador shoved backwards, and the stone popped loose from the dirt. He hit his head as he landed on the bones and rocks behind him. Pain wracked his body, both from the blow to his head and the sense of fire that exploded through him as if his very blood burned. The world faded away into inky blackness.

Struggling to get air beneath its massive wings, the large blue dragon gave another powerful thrust to gain height. The lance deep within its side made it difficult to draw air. It needed to land somewhere out of reach of the hunters. Seeing a small clearing upon the hillside, hidden by an overhanging ledge, the dragon wheeled about, coasting slowly down to land. Its wing made his path and descent uncertain. It hit the ground without grace, the clearing shaking from the hard landing. Unaware of the large boulder above, shaken from its resting, the dragon reached back with its large maw to grab a hold of the lance and jerk it free. It roared in pain, the fearsome sound echoing clear across the vale. The dragon reared back in response to the pain of the wound, its tail slamming into the cliff face behind it. The trembling earth, unsteady above the dragon, unleashed a torrent of rock that came slamming down, forcing the dragon to its knees beneath. A boulder pinned one of its wings to the ground, and the dragon roared out again. Weakened from the blood that flowed freely from the wound left by the lance; the dragon dropped its great head to the ground with a thud. Its last thought was not that it would die here, but something far nobler...

"SAVE THE FLEDGLINGS!"

"Alador...Alador..."

The feeling of gentle tapping against his cheek was strangely irritating. Alador's eyes fluttered open, but the light hurt and he squinted as the sea of faces danced above him. He groaned and put a hand to his aching head. He was still somewhat lost in the dream. It was as if he'd *been* the dragon, feeling its pain and its anxiety.

"What...happened?" He managed to moan more than speak. A strange dull thud seemed to be resounding in his head.

"You made the find of the turn, Alador, that's what happened. Oh, and...well, you hit your head pulling it out." Mesiande's excited voice sent his mind sailing back to the memory of the glistening bloodstone. He forced his eyes to focus and looked about frantically, but the stone was cradled in Mesiande's arms like a baby. His eyes met hers with worried concern.

"Such a large find! I am sure that you will be sharing a drink for all at the alehouse tomorrow, hey Alador?" Mesiande's tone made it clear that she would not be keeping secret whose stone this really was. The disgruntled look on Potre's face verified that this discussion must have taken place while he was out. Potre was the large man that led the team of miners into the hills to find dragon skeletons. He was almost an elder, but since he still could move like an adult, he hadn't chosen to move to the inner circle. His face was round and ruddy – a combination of age and weather as well as too much food and drink.

"Oh yes, the drinks will be on me," He added swiftly, knowing that it would help soften the miners' mood to know that plenty of drink awaited them without a slip from their own pockets.

Gradually the smiles spread, and Termet, another miner, leaned over and offered Alador a hand up. Termet, to his credit, had never asked or demanded Alador's larger stones. He was a robust man with hardened hands and a miner's build. He hardly ever spoke, but his manner was always kind. Alador accepted and swayed lightly on his feet as dizziness filled him. There was a strange pain in his rib, but nothing was there when Alador lifted his shirt. Mesiande brought his stone to him, and he took it with such gentleness that it might have been a swaddling babe. It was easily large enough to keep him in style for a year – perhaps large enough that Alador could afford to put up his own cottage when he entered manhood. When he looked back up, Alador realized that he and Mesiande were alone. The others, inspired by his find, were already digging frantically.

Alador stood there in somewhat of a daze. His head was pounding, and he still felt as if he was on fire inside. "Mesi, I'm still not feeling well. If you want to finish my claim, I think I have enough for today." He smiled at her, for where there was one large stone, usually there was a multitude of smaller ones. He knew that she would gladly take his dig.

Mesiande flashed him a conspiring grin and nodded. "Here, let me get you some shade first." She hung her cloak over some discarded bones and fashioned him a tiny bit of shade. Alador sank into the shadowed space thankfully. With the sun no longer blazing in his eyes, his headache eased slightly. Only when she saw him safely settled did Mesiande rush off to get her tools from her own hole.

Alador stared into his bloodstone after she left – it was different from the other large stones he'd seen. Usually there was a darkness to them that seemed to swirl and dance. This one was clear, like glass – Alador could hold it up and see through it. Odd…he could have sworn it was dark when he'd first uncovered it. Maybe it had just appeared dark and murky in the dirt. He hoped the change didn't reduce its value. As he stared into it, Alador slowly recalled the strange vision of the dragon. The dream had seemed so real, as if he'd stood within the dragon's body itself, to see the events unfold. The very recollection sent a stabbing pain under his ribs again, like it had been Alador who'd taken the lance wound. He rubbed it, but nothing was there.

He sat holding the stone, leaning back against the large bone, and closed his eyes. His head pounded still, and every strike of a miner's hammer seemed to make it worse. He still felt unusually warm, too, like the blood pounding in his head and veins was too hot. Slowly, he slipped back into unconsciousness, something pulling him far beyond the realms of his surroundings.

"It is time. We have not sought a dragonsworn in centuries." The blue dragon rose up its head in determination as it faced the other seven flight leaders. *"I*

know you have doubts. I know you have concerns, but our fledglings number less and less each turn. So this is what I propose: I will find us one I think is worthy of our gifts. Each flight will test him, and if that flight finds him worthy, it will share its knowledge and gifts. More and more of our fledglings will become safe again with each test he passes."

The red dragon rose up on its haunches, eyeing the group with arrogant disgust. "I say we kill the mortals, every one of them, and **then** *our fledglings will be safe." He snarled. Four of the other flight lieges answered with an approving roar. "Your love of mortals is senseless, Renamaum!"*

"That has been your philosophy for some time now, Keensight, yet you have only brought the mortals to anger and now they hunt with even more vigor. The mortals now see us as a resource in these lands. They seek our blood, bonded to the earth in our deaths. They seek our meat and our bones. Our fledglings are raised in captivity only to be killed for what will fall from the ground beneath them. In some places, they are bled almost to death...healed and bled once more. It is your hunting that has brought this to pass. No, we need a mortal who can speak for us." Renamaum's gaze held challenge as he looked to each flight liege.

The indecision between the flights was clear, and the blue dragon rose up and roared for silence as the large cavern rumbled beneath their roars and stamping. "I will find one and give my test, if he passes the Blue Fight's test, it will be for each flight in turn to decide if they will accept him. MY FLEDGLINGS will survive." He came down on all fours in anger. The cavern grew silent other than the hissing breaths of the great beasts. The blue dragon heaved his body around and left the gathering. He took to the air, angered by the lack of foresight in his cousins.

He soared on the wind, letting the cold air wash over him. Slowly his angered ebbed as he made a turn to ensure the path to his mate's cavern was safe. He did not see the war machine carefully covered in vines. He did not sense the mortals, hidden by magic from his sight. His first warning was the large lance that landed deep between two ribs. He roared in pain and warning and banked hard to the left; he fluttered and floundered purposely, letting the mortals give chase. His initial thought was of his mate, but he also gradually realized that his own situation was dire. If he hoped to save his fledglings, he would need to land and remove the vile wood within him. If he hoped to find the dragonsworn, he must survive this wound. He cast about for a safe place...

"Alador, come on lad, time for us to be gettin' back. You gonna make it?" Potre's voice almost sounded hopeful that Alador would not. The miner's greedy eyes were fixed upon the stone in Alador's lap.

"Yeah, sorry, must have dozed off." Alador opened his eyes to see the light was fading. He must have dozed off for some time. He fumbled the stone a little trying to work it into his bag. His head still hurt fiercely.

Once he was finally packed and ready to join the others, Mesiande hurried over to him and gave him a big hug.

"I found four others of good weight and several small jewelry pieces. I will have earned my keep this trip." She hugged Alador again. "Thank you…you didn't have to share your claim."

"I honestly didn't feel well enough to have dug more," Alador muttered. His mind was still caught in the strange dream. It must have been sleeping against the dragon bones that brought up such strangeness. Regardless of that – or the lump on his head – Alador was glad to leave this place. A dragon grave had never bothered him before, but now he felt like they shouldn't be there. He felt as if something was watching.

Mesiande took his hand to guide him down the path to where the korpen waited. She and Alador had shared a beast on the way here, and for once he was glad that he would not be riding alone on the way back. Usually he bemoaned the fact that neither of them could afford their own beast. The korpen's large back made two riders possible, just not comfortable. Usually their back spikes were only placed well enough for one rider's comfort. He'd found the ride up slightly nerve racking; one spike had been in the small of his back for most of the trip. Mesiande had padded it, but he'd worried more than once that the korpen would rear up and impale him.

Korpen had originally been slow moving pests that travelled in herds and acted as a nuisance to outlying farms. They were single-minded when hungry, despite their slow moving methodical pace. In untamed areas, korpen were wild and yet would still let you walk right up to them as they ate. Taming them was easy if they knew that a source of food awaited them. Their massive heads had double, vertically-oriented horns. The upper horn curved forward from behind the head, while the lower emerged from the head itself. As a protection from predators such as dragons, the spikes along their backs were almost impenetrable. That was useful to the miners: korpen were strong and a great amount of weight could be attached to each spike. Even as tall as he was, Alador could barely see over the back of one of the beasts.

The slope was steep. They slid their way back down to the beasts' tie line. Once there, Mesiande readied the animal and then climbed up first and scooted back. Alador looked at her, puzzled. "I...I thought you said a lady should always ride in front."

Mesiande grinned. "I felt you squirming all the way here. Besides, with that egg on your head, I don't want you falling off and taking me with you."

Alador started to argue, but realized she was probably right: he was still terribly tired, and his head hurt enough that he planned to seek out the healer when they returned. He let Mesiande help him up onto the beast's back, and when the rest were loaded, they fell into step. It would take a few hours to return to the small village nestled down by the water. While korpen were resilient and could cover any terrain, they were not a mount for speed...and they didn't go straight down a hill. A slow switchback system had to be used to keep them moving forward. A korpen wouldn't move at all if it was pointed straight up or down a hill.

They had not made the second switch back before Alador faded back into unconsciousness.

Chapter Two

It was two days before Alador was well enough to leave the healer's hut. Fortunately, his smaller stone had paid for his care, and he hadn't been forced to once again beg for funds from his brother and the smithy. Many villagers had come to see Alador's find, but the healer hadn't let them bother him. So it came as no surprise, as he stepped into the bright sunlight, blinking quickly against the glare, that half the village was waiting outside to see this rumored bloodstone. Alador shifted uncomfortably as Potre came up and put a large fleshy arm around him. Alador had always been the one left on the outside of the circle, and now that so many expectant gazes fell to him, he couldn't help but wish he had kept the stone a secret somehow. He was uncomfortable in the silence that settled, standing in front of so many people as Potre grabbed ahold of him.

Potre's voice rang out loudly. "Come on lad, let them see it." Potre acted as if they'd always been friends, even though up till now he'd barely tolerated Alador's presence.

Alador nodded and knelt down, carefully untied his mining sack, and pulled the large stone out. He held it high up over his head for all those waiting to see. The gasps of pleasure and surprise were somehow gratifying, despite his discomfort. Alador lowered the stone and walked out into the midst of those gathered. Many of those who'd previously shunned him now patted him on the back, and more than one caressed the stone. Alador was overwhelmed by the attention, the comments, and the constant touching of those about him. It was as if he was the luck pole, and each one needed to touch him or the stone. Finally his oldest brother, Dorien, came to his rescue.

"All right, I'm taking him home. You've all seen enough. Alador just left the healer's hut; give the poor boy some space." Dorien put an arm around Alador, grabbed his mining sack, and began to move him out of the circle.

Dorien hadn't often touched Alador kindly in the past; Alador had always felt like the child not quite wanted even in his own home. To have his brother take him in the shelter of those large blacksmith arms and guide him home was more of a shock to Alador than the village reactions. He realized that, despite the unfamiliarity, he was grateful for the protection from the many eyes that followed them.

"Dorien, why all this fuss over a bloodstone?" Alador asked as they approached the stoop of their home. The house had always amused him; it was as if each room had been added as an afterthought. The stairs to the upper floors had been built along the outside because the rooms within were too small to accommodate them. It was a maze that the small ones loved for games of hiding. The best things about the house, though, were the building's rich hues of brown and cream, the smell of his maman's cooking, and the warmth that filled its walls. Even with his status as a half-breed, his home was still one filled with love…well, between sibling fights and his maman's scolding.

"Alador, have you no idea what your stone might fetch?" Dorien looked at him with a calculating gaze.

"Well, knowing what I get for the small bloodstones, I thought it might be enough for this year's upkeep for myself, maybe a little extra to take care of a woman's small ones, someday," Alador admitted, not quite sure. "I've never seen one so large, so…I'm not even sure if it might not be just too big." He stared at the stone. It was heavy, and he could see through it like red window glass, although its thickness distorted the image somewhat. He held it up and gazed through it as they paused outside.

"Alador, you'll never have to mine again if you don't want to. Your stone will fetch enough for a lifetime! It'll put you in the same graces as Ketchen, at least." Ketchen had made his slips by an invention to a plow he had created. Every blacksmith including Dorien had paid him a great deal to get the specifications for the plow head. Even Lerdenian smiths had come to learn the design – it could deepen the furrow and was less inclined to bind with the spring grass, and it had given him enough slips to choose his craft and build the nicest house in the village. Alador looked up in surprise at his brother. He'd spent many a time envying Ketchen, who always seemed to be in the alehouse or out on his stoop.

Dorien looked at Alador. "You'll likely have every woman competing for your attention now, despite your…father's race."

Alador stopped walking and turned to face his brother. "I...I do...what will I do?"

Dorien's deep laugh boomed, apparently alerting their mother to their arrival. "You must be the only middlin in town who does not dream of a day where he does not have to toil for his keep."

Their conversation was interrupted by their mother, Alanis, rushing out to take Alador in her arms. "I was so afraid we lost you!" She checked him over quickly, which caused his brothers and sisters to laugh. They pulled him into the main room of the house, where Alador found a meal laid out for him. His mother pushed him into a chair; ever since Alador could remember, her philosophy was that food would cure all ailments. Dorien took the stone from his hands and placed it in the center of the table.

Tentret, who was also older than Alador, stared at it. "I have never seen one so clear."

Alador paused from shoveling cream soup into his mouth. "That's what I thought...the stone is so clear, I fear it will lower its value."

"Or raise it," offered his little sister, Sofie, hopefully.

"Even if it lowers the value, I doubt you will feel the loss overmuch, Alador," Dorien offered, turning a chair so he could rest his chin on the back as he straddled it.

"We should get a drawing of it before you sell it." Tentret ran to fetch his drawing things, and worked a quick sketch of Alador eating with the stone in front of him. It would allow the family to keep a record of how large the bloodstone really was.

"I bet it has all the power of the entire dragon in it," Sofie offered. "An enchanter would pay dearly for such a gift. I would, if I could wield the magic—"

Sofie's words were cut off as their mother backhanded her off the chair with a firm scolding. "Daezun don't soil their souls with the twisting of magics. We leave such risks to Lerdenians. I had best never hear such foolishness from your mouth again." Maman was usually a kind of hovering sort of mother until the talk of magic was brought up. It was odd, given that she had taken Alador's father Henrick to her ritual furs. The mage seemed to have a way of making her forget her hatred of such things, but it only intensified when he departed. Despite already knowing how she would react to the topic, Alador still winced when his mother backhanded Sofie.

"Yes Maman." Sofie wiped her mouth clear of the specks of blood shed from biting her lip. "I didn't mean no harm."

"Look how hard your brother has had it, looking like his father. No man will care for your small ones if you be talking such nonsense," Maman continued her scolding, her small hands now on her hips.

Alador rolled his eyes, and his brother chuckled as their mother began her favorite threat. He wiped the last of the soup out of the bowl with a piece of bread loaf. Ever since Alador could remember, his heritage had been used in comparison for why or why not a particular action should be considered. The only time he ever saw any difference in the scorn of his Lerdenian blood was when his father came to visit. The enchanter softened something in Alanis, and she spoke not a word of ill will against his heritage. Alador often wondered if the enchanter had cast some spell on her so that she'd choose him in the circle – she'd become giddy, almost like a middlin again, whenever the mage was in the village.

Sofie's eyes glistened with tears she dare not shed here; Daezun women did not cry – only small ones cried. Alador flashed Sophie a sympathetic glance. She'd recently had her woman's time, and would go into the circle this year as a result, though she didn't speak of that much. Alador knew there was a part of her that longed to leave the village, and that had been something her siblings teased her about a great deal. Only traders ever left the village, and everyone knew that traders were the worst kind of folk. In many ways, Sofie was still a young middlin. Unfortunately, she was not allowed to act as one any longer. Alador did feel sympathetic: though she was fully Daezun, Sofie's dreams did not fit the Daezun way.

"Maman, do you think I could have some more?" Alador asked, holding up his empty bowl. He was so hungry; a strange gnawing tugged at his belly like he hadn't eaten for days. Besides, it would help take the attention off of Sofie. His sister whispered a wordless thank you as their mother turned to look at Alador.

True to form, Maman grabbed up the dish to hurry off to the stove. Focused on Alador again, she let Sofie be. "Of course, my dear, of course, you surely haven't been fed a measure of decent food in that blasted healer's hut. When you're full, I've arranged a bath in the hothouse for you." His mother bustled about like a mother hen.

Alador wrinkled his nose. "A bath?" The hothouse had been built around a natural spring. The fires in the house kept it warm, and the water came from the ground at a fair temperature in any case, but Alador hadn't ever liked bathing in it. He was different from the other men, and one rarely used the house alone. He didn't like thinking about the comments that were made about his body – none of them were complimentary. He definitely didn't feel like being singled out any more today.

Tentret chuckled as he drew. He knew full well why Alador did not like the baths. But, as usual, his brother said nothing; he only continued his deft sketching. Alador flashed him a pleading look, but Tentret ignored him. Alador was apparently on his own for this one.

"Yes! A bath!" His mother took on a familiar tone, one Alador knew would be useless to argue against. "First, you have a healer's stench about you. Second, I seen how you're walking. The soaking will do your body good. I even have some meraweed for the fire." Her eyes met his in a firm, reproaching way, and Alador obediently looked down as she set the bowl of soup in front of him.

"Yes Maman." If she were parting with meraweed, he dared not dig his heels in against her. Meraweed had a strange property that relaxed the body and made it difficult to track time. It seemed to help in healing wounds and illnesses. Alador wondered if it would help with the odd pain in his ribs, or the sensation that his very blood burned. It had eased a little over the last two days, but Alador still felt it when he stopped to think about it.

"Good; it's settled, then. Sofie, run and fetch your brother a drying cloth and a fresh set of clothes." Alador did not look up as he ate. He already knew – and Sofie's quick intake of breath reminded him – that it was an insult to be sent to wait on him. He usually did the running for all the others. Alador sat and wondered about this sudden change that overcame even in his mother. He had never seen slips as all that significant to the way things were.

Alador didn't look up again till Dorien spoke: "After you're done with that bath and your head clears Alador, stop by the forge. I think we need to talk about a couple things." Dorien's tone also left no room for argument, and by the look that passed between him and their mother, Alador knew they were up to something.

"Yes, Dorien," Alador responded quietly, he watched as his brother stood up and swung the chair back around the right way. It was one of the things he admired in his brother: there was a commanding air about him – an easy confidence. His eyes often sparkled when he was up to something. He was also often sought after in the circle.

"I'll be off, then. Josen wants that plow head on the morrow, and it isn't quite right yet." Dorien picked up the stone off the table. "Folks will be expecting you to hide this here. I'll take it over to the forge in the wheelbarrow and hide it well."

Alador nodded and glanced at Tentret who was still sketching. Apparently he had enough done, because he didn't argue when his brother scooped up the bloodstone and strode out. Tentret earned his keep with sketches and paintings. It was a rare skill in a village, and many had come to his brother for house pictures, sketches of new tools and buildings, and other things of that nature. Tentret had a way of knowing what something should look like by the way someone else described it. However, Alador also knew Tentret wouldn't show it to him until it met his own satisfaction.

Alador was just finishing the second bowl of soup when Sofie came hurrying back into the room. She laid the neat bundle tied with twine upon the table. His mother slipped a pouch containing the meraweed onto the top of the bundle. She was pulling the bowl out of under him even as he put his last spoonful into his mouth.

"Best you get over there." She nodded towards the door.

"I'm a little tired Maman," Alador offered in hopes of getting out of a bath. He really had no desire to sit in the hothouse and be the spectacle for others to whisper about, nor did he want to be drawn into conversation about the bloodstone.

"All the more reason to go soak in the spring and rest there," Maman replied. "Besides, Sofie and I have work, and you'll just be in the way." She practically pulled Alador from the chair and shoved him out the door, thrusting the bundle into his arms as he stepped out. His mother was not a small woman by any measure.

Alador sighed with resignation and trudged slowly towards the hothouse. The last thing he wanted to do was run into Trelmar and his friends at the bath. Trelmar had made Alador's life miserable for as long as he could remember. He seemed to find happiness in it. He was the same number of turns as Alador, and had always outsized him. Alador had lost count of how many times he'd taken a beating, had his head stuffed into the dung bin, or been cast into the prickleberries thanks to Trelmar and his friends.

Alador opened the hothouse door only barely enough to peek inside, and was relieved to see it empty. He carefully undressed, folding his clothes as he went and then hiding them from plain sight – a tactic he had long ago learned to keep from having to come out of the bath without clothes. Trelmar had stolen them more than once.

Once his clothes were hidden, Alador placed his meraweed in the fire that the village kept smoldering at all times. The small, darkened room slowly filled with the plant's relaxing vapor. With an easy smile, Alador went to the pool and slipped into it. Meraweed was given out in only small quantities by the healer. Apparently if too much of it was used, it made people lose focus on day-to-day events, preferring instead to spend all of their time in the hothouse. Alador could see why: a sense of peace and sleepiness quickly washed over him. He had to admit, his mother had been right. Alador already felt much better, and he soon lost track of time as the water soothed his aches and pains away – even the strange pain in his side for which he could not account.

Alador didn't know how long he had been half-sleeping in the spring. Long ago, the spring had been lined with stones and small seats created, making the bath comfortable to doze in without fear of drowning. The sound of the door opening breached Alador's awareness. So much for the privacy he had been enjoying. He didn't open his eyes until he heard the grating voice that brought a cringe to his very core:

"Ah, the village idiot-turned-hero." The tone held a cold edge of hate.

Alador opened his eyes to see his own personal nightmare standing before him with a sarcastic grin. Trelmar's arms were crossed, and the fire behind him created an ominous silhouette. Of course, Trelmar had three of his lackeys with him. Alador pretended not to notice who Trelmar was speaking to as the four of them stripped down and hopped into the spring with him. He was glad it was large; maybe they would just stay on their own side. The meraweed was fading, so Alador would leave once they were settled.

"No words from our 'hero,' eh?" Trelmar needled some more. "Doesn't change anything. Put a fine bridle on a Korpen, but it still won't fly. Put fine clothes on the village buffoon; he'll still be a joke."

Anger began to seethe within Alador. He knew better than to speak, or risk another beating – and he was still feeling odd. He dare not try to take on the four of them. "I'll leave you the bath," Alador snarled out, knowing he'd have to get out in front of them. At least it was better than staying in with them.

"Oh, don't leave. Why, everyone is in awe of the great miner, Aladork." Trelmar's mocking tone echoed off the water, giving it a hollow sound.

Alador hissed in anger but got up anyway and turned to crawl out of the pool. He wasn't quick enough. Hands grabbed him and pulled him backwards and under the water. Alador thrashed about as hands seemed to come from everywhere, holding him under the water, keeping him from being able to breathe. Time seemed to slow as he struggled to get free of those holding him just short of reaching air. He finally managed to break free and grab air just when he thought he would pass out, only to be shoved under again. Every time Alador came up, gasping for air, they would shove him back under the water. He swung his fists madly, but it didn't take long for them to grab his arms and render him helpless. Panic and rage swept through him. Would they really kill him? Alador's lungs burned – he needed air. He fought for all he was worth as the fire in his lungs coursed to his very blood.

His thrashing – and the efforts of Trelmar and his friends to hold him beneath the surface – hid the bubbles that began to rise around Alador. The room filled with the sounds of the boys' laughter and the thrashing of limbs in water. The steam increased until the boys could hardly see one another, then suddenly, the hands were gone. Alador came up gasping for air, and the boys' malicious laughter had turned to screams of pain. Alador's first few ragged gasps were precious. In anger, he turned, wanting to hit whoever was closest to him, then whipped around again, watching in confusion as his assailants fled, screaming, from the pool. They turned to stare at Alador, who stood gasping for air, chest-deep in the center of the bath, water bubbling around him and steam obscuring his vision. He screamed in fury and outrage, the sound bestial in its intensity. Alador was so scared and angry. He wanted nothing more than to get his hands on Trelmar and rip him limb from limb.

The assailants snatched up their clothes and ran from the hothouse naked and screaming. Alador looked about him in a daze. Why had they left off? Why had they run? He slowly worked his way to the edge, still panting for air, and then crawled out of the pool and sat with his drying cloth against his face in confusion. He stayed that way while his anger slowly dulled. Alador knew that if he stepped out after Trelmar now, he would just earn another beating; it was unlikely Alador would win. He never had been able to best the cruel middlin.

Alador slowly dried himself and dressed. Gathering up his dirty clothes, he set off numbly towards the smithy. He didn't understand why Trelmar and his lackeys had left off and run as they did. He just thanked the gods – which ever ones had been watching over him.

Dorien looked up as Alador approached. He nodded to a stool as he hammered away on the plow head he was working. Alador, despite his dislike for the work here, still loved to come to the smithy. The forge was rarely cooled. He'd spent many an hour working the bellows, while his brothers worked the metal. Even now, Tentret was molding something on an anvil. The forge sat under a covered roof, high above them. It had a face that opened up outside where the two men worked now, but it could also be used from the inside during colder weather. The bellows were off to the side within. It was a hot job in the summer, but a pleasant one in the winter. Large barrels of water were set about for cooling, but there were also buckets close by in case of fire.

Alador set his clothes beside the stool and hopped up. He watched as Dorien worked on the finishing touches, buffing the metal smooth – he hadn't added the handles yet. It was a straight plow, used for heavy plowing, and Dorien worked on the top that would be added to the plow beam. When he was finally pleased with the current work and the metal cooled too much to continue, Dorien put down his hammer. He ducked his head into one of the barrels, shaking the water off like a big beast before turning with a grin to approach Alador. He wiped his wet face on a sleeve, spreading more black soot than he had removed.

He motioned for Alador to walk with him – Tentret's hammering was too loud to talk over. Once they were far enough away from the smithy, Dorien began to speak. "While you were ill in the healer's hut, there was a lot of talk about your future. Your find will help you overcome your curse of blood. While you may not be ever chosen at the mating circle, it is possible that many will want you to help raise their small ones. The elders decided you should join the ritual circle this year rather than the usual age. It will give you a chance to establish a life and not wait with too much coin to spend." Dorien glanced over at Alador to see his brother's reaction, and chuckled at his open, gaping-mouthed expression. "Don't be so surprised; there have been others allowed in the circle at a younger age, if circumstances dictated it was proper."

The ritual circle was the mating tradition of the Daezun people. Small ones and those too old for mating created an inner circle around a large circular tent filled with furs and blankets, and those in this circle sat with their backs to the nest behind them. They were the musicians for the circle. The drumming had always been Alador's favorite part of this ritual. He had ventured a glance once or twice to the activities behind him, but he never saw very much. The next circle out was for the women of mating age – they danced about in ways that still brought color to Alador's face. The outer circle was for the men they could choose from as the night progressed. Daezun lived to be about one hundred eighty turns, but they weren't usually allowed into the mating circle until thirty turns as males, or whenever they had their woman's time for females – usually between twenty-four and thirty-two turns.

There were more men than women in a Daezun village, so there were always a variety of men that a woman could choose. These men danced also, but in the opposite direction. You could always tell who was new to the circle; newer dancers tended to shuffle about more than actually dancing. The ritual continued until the drummers could drum no longer. Rumor said that the women drank a potion to keep them going; Alador could believe it, with as long as this mating continued. Sometimes, women chose more than one man as the night progressed. The ritual was always held at the height of the summer, usually on the shortest night of the turn. This way, the babies were born right before spring planting and most of the work for women was still light.

Alador was not prepared for the news – he was to be allowed into this year's circle! His mind raced as he tried to fathom what his brother was saying to him, and he'd stopped walking. "I...I...What am I to do?" He knew there was some kind of ritual or meeting that men attended before the ritual. He knew the location of the small house that was used – he had seen others leave it after their ritual to become an adult. That was about the extent of what he knew.

Dorien flashed a wicked grin. "Oh, we'll make sure you know what you need to," he promised. There was a mischievous twinkle in his gaze that concerned Alador.

It was then that their mother came running up. "Alador, are you whole?" She grabbed Alador's hands and flipped them palm-up, then down. She grabbed his head and searched his face worriedly.

"Maman, the boy is about to be brought into the circle of men. Stop treating him like a small one, by the gods, you're even embarrassing me," Dorien scolded, but he eyed Alador, too, looking for some mysterious wound.

"The other lads came out of the hot house burnt up," she answered, tugging up Alador's shirt. "The water spiked hot and scalded them good."

"Maman!" Alador shoved his shirt back down. "I'm fine!" He batted her hands away before she started after his trousers. "I'm fine. I...I got out before I got burned," he offered. He flushed, not used to lying to his mother. Well it wasn't exactly a lie. He *had* gotten out, and he wasn't burned. He still wasn't quite sure why they were burned and he wasn't, but at least he knew now why they had fled like they had. Still, Alador was not about to let his mother undress him here on the path before all and sundry.

She stepped back, staring at him. "But...they said you were still in the water. We ran to fetch you out, but then you weren't there." She looked him over. "Are you sure you're all right?"

"They must have thought I was still in. I was on the other side of the bath, there was a lot of steam," Alador answered somewhat absently. He was fairly sure that Trelmar wouldn't say how he 'knew' that Alador had been in the pool, or he'd have to admit what they had been doing. What Alador didn't understand was how he managed to emerge unscathed. He'd been in the thick of them; if they'd been burned, he should have been, too.

Alador let his mother fuss over him all the way back to the house; his only protest was a look to his brother, who just laughed and waved them goodbye. He heard something about going to bed and resting, and he just nodded mutely as his mother shooed him up the outside stairs to the attic room he shared with Tentret. His mind was too lost in that moment when the four had left the bath. He plopped down on his small bed, and stared at the roughhewn beams and thatch above him. Why hadn't Alador been burned? The pool did warm up every once in a while, sometimes getting too hot to use, but he couldn't remember it suddenly heating up. Why had he not felt it? These questions kept haunting Alador until, finally, he fell asleep.

Chapter Three

Alador got up early in the morning and slipped out of the house with his bow. He hadn't seen Mesiande since he'd woken up in the healer's hut yesterday, and he knew she would be out at the practicing fields with Gregor. Gregor was in the same year of small ones as Alador, and Mesiande was a year behind them. They had remained firm friends throughout the years and, if Alador were being honest with himself, Gregor and Mesiande were the only two people in the village he could entirely trust. They had a tendency to sneak out in the mornings to spend time together, since their chores usually took them in different directions throughout the day.

Outside the village, the fields were worked in three parts – two for the village crops, and one to leave fallow – which spiraled around the village each planting season. The practice targets were always in the fallow fields. Sure enough, Alador found both of his friends with their bows, working on their targets. Daezun rarely did battle since the treaty had been established with Lerdenia, but everyone old enough to fight was expected to know how to use their weapon. One never knew when the peace they enjoyed would fade away.

The morning dew was still fresh on the grass beneath Alador's feet, and a slight fog rose up from the fields, giving them a mystical appearance. The sun was barely peeking over the hill, and the first rays of its warmth bathed him. The morning air smelled of fresh dirt, breakfast from the village, and – unfortunately – a little bit of korpen dung. A light breeze ruffled Alador's hair as he moved across the fields towards the practice area. It was going to be a beautiful day.

Alador grinned as he came down the steps to the fallow field. Mesiande was clearly scolding Gregor on his stance – again. It was something both he and Gregor were familiar with. Alador had to admit it: of the three of them, Mesiande was far better with a bow. She was standing just behind Gregor's draw with her hands on her hips, in the position she'd always taken when she was frustrated with either of them. It was one of the things Alador loved about her; she was so cute when she was angry. He had learned not to laugh – it always made her angrier – but Mesiande made it hard on him. She would always wrinkle her nose and stomp her little foot. It was adorable.

When she heard him approach, Mesiande turned. Alador had just enough time to drop his bow before she flung herself into his arms to embrace him fiercely. Alador caught her and spun her about. He loved her hugs, and she gave them freely.

"You're all right!" she cried.

Alador held her short, stocky frame in the air, smiling down at her rosy cheeks. "I am fine, Mesi," he assured her. He looked over to see Gregor approaching, and set Mesiande down to clasp forearms with him.

"Thought yah was gonna be addlebrained there, Alador. But then I thought, by the gods, wouldn't be any

different," Gregor teased. His build was heavier than
Alador's, and he had a smile that lit his eyes and and a
kindness that exceeded any other Daezun that Alador
knew. Even when things were in strife, Gregor had an
amenable look about him.

Alador, in response, jerked Gregor forward and
twisted so that Gregor landed on his back. Alador quickly
placed a knee against him, holding him down. "For
someone who's addled, I can still put you down easily
enough!" They both laughed, and Alador helped Gregor
back to his feet.

"I just let yah win, yah know that," Gregor fired
back as he got up. There might have been truth to that,
though Alador made up in agility what Gregor had in
strength.

Alador smiled at his friend. "Say what you must
to soothe that pride of yours," he quipped. The three
laughed as they walked back to the makeshift shooting
range where Mesiande and Gregor had discarded their
bows.

When they arrived, Mesiande cheerfully picked up
her bow. "You might want to wait, Al. We're working the
farthest target." She flashed him a look of apology.

Alador frowned. One thing he'd apparently
inherited from his father, other than unusual color of his
eyes, was his poor eyesight. "Well, I'd still like to try.
Maybe I can at least hit it, even if it isn't a kill
shot." Alador sat down on a rock, readied his bow, and
checked his fletching. Due to his height, his bow had
been specially made for him by his brother for a little
extra reach. Years of helping in the smithy had kept
Alador strong enough to compete with his stockier
friends.

He waited until both had taken a couple shots, then stepped to the practice line. He sighted down the shaft of his arrow and, for a brief moment, it seemed as if the target was just a few yards in front of him. Alador lifted his head and blinked a couple of times. The target became a blur on the field. He shook his head and sighted down the arrow once more. There it was again, the target looming right in front of him. He lifted his head and, yet again, the target was a blur in the far off distance.

"Can't you even see it, Alador?" asked Mesiande curiously. "You could at least see it before you hit your head. Maybe you hurt yourself more than you thought." She moved to his side with a bit of concern.

"No...no, I can see it," Alador murmured. "I was just...umm...double checking." He sighted once more, and this time when the target appeared before him, he fired into the circles painted there.

"By the gods," gasped Mesiande. "I think you hit it!" She shielded her eyes against the morning sun with a hand to get a better look.

"He did!" Gregor danced around the other side of Alador. "Bet yah can't do it twice!"

"Probably not." Alador strung another arrow. "I'm sure it was luck." He sighted in again, but centered himself this time, and when the target jumped towards him, he fired. He stood in amazement as the arrow flew straight to the target's center. He eyed the target, but it seemed like a blur again now that he wasn't focused. What was going on? Alador looked to Mesiande as she spoke.

"Dead on...I'm sure of it." She looked at Alador in awe. "Or maybe that hit in the head fixed your sight?" She looked at him with large eyes, and Alador felt a wave of pride and pleasure sweep over him.

"Let's go get our arrows and see." Gregor was excited as he scooped up his bow.

The three took a walk out to the target. Mesiande and Gregor were laughing, joking and pushing as they went. Alador was unusually quiet, though, lost in his thoughts. The target's movement had unsettled him. He felt different, too, but if he were asked, Alador wouldn't know how to explain the difference. His head didn't hurt, and he felt well enough, but something was definitely off. He glanced at Mesiande, laughing with Gregor, and felt a moment of irritation that they were both ignoring him.

Mesiande's blue-fletched arrows were all well placed in the center circle. Gregor's black fights were more sporadic, but all of his shots would still have caused a damaging blow if the target had been a man. Alador's two blue flights were far apart, one just outside the target circle, the other dead-center. A perfect shot. Mesiande reached up and caressed it, awestruck. "I have never seen you place a perfect shot on any but the close target, Al." She looked over at him.

"I'm sure it was just…a lucky shot," Alador murmured. What was happening around him? First the baths, then this strange ability. Then there were the odd dreams of the blue dragon, like he'd been the one in the dragon's body. Had Alador done permanent damage when he hit his head?

"Well, let's go find out." Mesiande pulled Alador's arrows and then her own, letting Gregor fend for himself. They spent some time practicing, and Alador put a center shot in the targets again and again, missing only when Mesiande poked him right as he fired. Each time, the target seemed to zoom in when he focused down his arrow. They practiced till the work bell sounded.

Each day that they were not out bloodstone mining, they had other tasks; today was one of those days. Mesiande helped in her mother's field or worked in the ore mine. Gregor was learning his house father's trade of building, and Alador, of course, helped in the smithy. They gathered up their things and headed back to the village.

"I think it is great that you can see better," Mesiande offered.

"Yeah, if I'd known hittin' yah in the head would be all it took, I would've clobbered yah harder a long time ago!" Gregor added helpfully.

Alador chuckled. "Thanks...I think." He looked over at his friend and forced a smile to his lips. He wanted to laugh and joke with them as usual, but he was perplexed by this new skill. He felt different. Not like he was still sick, but different, and he wasn't ready to share this with his two best friends.

They climbed to the top of the hill that lay between the village and the practice field, and Alador looked down toward the village. Despite feeling like an outsider all of his life, there was always something welcoming about the village. It was built in a layered circle, with the middle left open for visiting traders and celebrations like the mating ritual. The first ring contained buildings like the smithy and other craftsmen's shops. The next ring held the houses of the elders. Each had been carefully built and was of the nicest craftsmanship. Only those too old to bear small ones and work were allowed in the elder homes. During the day, the small ones were sent to this circle to learn the wisdoms and to be kept safe till they were old enough to work.

During the late afternoon when the sun wasn't so high, middlins like Alador and his friends would take groups of those almost old enough to leave the elder's teaching for small practice trips in the fields, to the smithy, or even to a small area set up to practice mining. After all, bloodstones weren't the only things worth mining. In the winter, skills such as fletching, skinning and spinning were taught. This time of preparation and trial allowed each small one to choose or be chosen for professions that suited them as he grew to become a middlin.

The next few rings of buildings were the houses of the other villagers, often not as fully-formed as the elder homes. Instead, they were added to as each household saw a need. Much like Alador's home, wings and extra floors sprang out and up as if just thrown on. All the houses had the same warm, rich, hewn beams and thatched roofs. Barrels were placed all around the village to catch rain water, but there was also a well for times without rain. From where Alador stood, the village looked like a wagon wheel, with all paths from the outer edges ending at the center circle.

The touch of a warm hand against his arm brought Alador out of his musing, and he looked down to see Mesiande peering at him with concern. Gregor had moved on without them, apparently. They stood alone in the light warm breeze.

"You hardly talked the entire time we were practicing, Alador." She searched his face. "I'm worried about you. Maybe you shouldn't work today? I'm pretty sure your family and the elders would understand." She moved her hand up his arm gently.

"I'm just...thinking, Mesi. There's nothing to worry about." Alador was suddenly very conscious of her touch upon his arm. He could feel the heat of her hand as it moved.

"Are you worried that Trelmar will come after you?" She looked around like she expected the middlin to appear at any moment.

"No." Alador blushed a deep red. No, his thoughts had definitely not been on Trelmar.

"Is it that you don't have to mine any more if you don't want to?" Mesiande could be a pest when she wanted to know something.

Alador sighed with exasperation. If he didn't tell her, she would just keep going until she figured it out. "Dorien told me today that I'll be joining the ritual this year because of the stone. Everyone is treating me differently than I'm used to because of that stone. I'm glad and all, but I...I don't know what I think or how I feel about all this. Confused, I guess. I'm not sure how to act." Alador's confession spilled out in a rush of words.

When he'd said he would enter the ritual, Alador thought for a moment he saw dismay on Mesiande's face, but then she smiled. "Well, of course they are. If it wasn't for your heritage, you'd probably be the most desired housemate at the yearly gathering. Even so, many will overlook it because of what the sale of that stone could mean for you. A few might have overlooked it anyway...you *are* rather pleasing to look upon." She bit her lip as she watched his face, her cheeks flushing a delicate pink.

"Now you're just being nice." Alador sighed and ran a hand through his short, drab hair in frustration. "I don't want to go to the mating circle without..." Now it was his turn to flush with color. "We'd better get to work." He strode down the hill now, not wanting to look at Mesiande. She followed him silently with a huge smile on her face, but did not try to stop him. They parted ways at the bottom of the hill, Mesiande toward the mines and Alador toward the smithy.

The next few days passed uneventfully. Trelmar had given him a wide berth once he'd been released from the healer's hut. An old, comfortable routine re-established itself. Alador and his friends worked their bows in the morning, did their village tasks till the learning bell, then took the small ones out to pick berries, learn to swim, or perform other simple tasks. Evenings were spent with family tasks, or, on occasion, hunting with Tentret or fishing with Gregor. The hunting and fishing had been outstanding since the snows had fallen off.

While many of the villagers still watched and whispered as he passed, Alador was becoming accustomed to this new kind of attention. The awkward moments were when someone actually took a moment to ask after his day. Alador would shuffle, murmur and disappear as quickly as he could without being rude. For years, he had complained that he was an outsider. Now that he had more acceptance, he realized just how much more peaceful life had been when he was on his own. In a way, Alador thought that this new attention still was a form of being on the outside – only now people cared if he also disliked them.

This routine continued till the traders' caravan came to town. It was a rare event for the caravan to visit, so there was always an outpouring of excitement when the villagers noticed the extra kicked-up dust on the road. The caravan would roll in, surrounded by armed guards as it moved, marking a day of celebration, feasting, music, and – of course – bartering. The caravan worked a route of Daezun settlements; each village excelled at differing crafts and then passed their wares on in the caravan. They also carried items from Lerdenia, which the villages found hard to acquire on their own. By the time all the the caravan had filtered in, the center of the village had become full of wagons-turned-stalls where the traders hawked their wares. At the very center, rough boards were set up as tables and benches, and a prang was set to roasting on a large spit. Middlins took turns keeping the wild beast turning and brushing it with a sweet sauce that brought out the meat's rich flavor.

Prang was available year-round, but it embodied the image of winter. Their white and brown coats made it easy for them to blend in with the dead foliage of the cold winter months. An adult prang could weigh up to two hundred and fifty stones – too large for individual families – so the village as a whole sometimes hunted them for their meat, or their horns for the healers. A prang's upswept and back-curving horns could be used in medicine for headaches and eyesight.

When they were done trading, the women became busy with cooking, and soon the boards filled with foods of all varieties. The traders always brought the drink to the table as their contribution, so that they could spend their time in trade and didn't have to worry about a meal when they were done.

While, on occasion, medure slips – the strange, rectangle pieces of metal that were the currency between Lerdenia and Daezun – changed hands, most of the trading was done by exchanging goods. Of course, traders always came out ahead in the bargains, but that was just the way of things. Medure was a hard metal that glistened with flecks of blue; it was difficult to find and harder to work. Most villagers didn't want to keep the slips – they often brought thieves. Some wouldn't trade at all if they couldn't barter fair goods straight across.

Dorien had suggested that Alador wait till the day was mostly done before heading over to the trader that bought bloodstones. He wouldn't be trading goods because the bloodstone trader worked with the Lerdenian Empire, and only had slips to give in trade. As Alador worked his way through the stalls, a crowd began to appear behind him, eager to see what the stone was worth. By the time he'd made it to the bloodstone trader's stall, he had a personal retinue of as many villagers as could fit into the small spaces and still see him.

Alador waited patiently as one of the other miners traded in an egg-sized stone. It brought fifty medure – a nice price for any miner. A single medure could get a great deal in trade goods. When the man had completed his trade, Alador stepped up. The crowd about him became quiet.

"Ah, I do not have to ask. You must be the young man with the hulking stone I keep hearing about." The man's smooth way of speaking was only outdone by the silken robes he wore. Alador had traded here before, so he was used to the odd appearance of the stone trader, but even so, he found himself at a loss for words. He just nodded.

Alador set the stone upon the weight board. He heard the sharp intake of the man's breath and looked up as the man stared at it. "It is clear...?" The trader tapped it curiously, watching Alador closely.

"I know. I hope it doesn't lower the value too much." Alador looked up at the taller man with concern, shifting fearfully. What if the trader didn't want it? He looked back to the stone and up to the trader again with evident anxiety.

The trader licked his dry lips and spoke, "Well, I do think I will be lowering the weight price a bit. I have never seen one that had the appearance of a window pane, red though it is." The trader stroked the smooth stone curiously.

"What do you offer then, sir?" Alador's hands were clenched tight. His brother, Dorien had worked his way to Alador's side and put a reassuring hand on his shoulder. He surely could get at least four hundred for it.

"Well, it is substantial to be sure. And its weight measure is the largest I have seen." The man pursed his lips and tapped his chin in thought. "I will offer you five hundred medure."

The crowd gasped about him, and the price was whispered back all over to those that could not hear. Alador was ecstatic. That was one hundred more than he had been hoping to receive. Before Alador could speak, his brother scooped up the stone. "I think we'll just make a trip to the border, Alador. I mean, why should you stand here and let this thief rob you? Five hundred is an insult."

Alador looked up at Dorien, wondering if his brother had lost his mind. He was more than happy with five hundred and was about to tell Dorien so when the trader raised a hand. "Wait! Wait now. Perhaps I have been a little hasty in my offering." Alador's eyes riveted to the trader's in disbelief. His mouth hung open with the weight of his shock. He had never considered that traders would undervalue the bloodstones. He had always just accepted what the men offered in the past. He had felt so grateful to have slips that he had focused on the things they would purchase.

"Well then, my friend, you'd best be giving a fairer accounting to my brother, or we will have no business to attend," Dorien answered imperiously. Alador looked over to his brother and was surprised to see a bit of anger in his expression. Dorien's usual jovial manner was gone as he drew himself up. The large size of the blacksmith made Alador look small beside him.

"One thousand medure, and that is fair! You would have to take time from your shop to go to the border for a better offer, otherwise." The trader fired back. He looked between the two brothers and bit his lip as he waited for Dorien's counter.

Dorien did not answer right away. "Five thousand and I might consider it an apology for an attempt at thievery." Dorien's tone left no room for argument, and he stood tense at his brother's side. He looked closely at the trader closely as if watching for something.

The man paused; his face flushed a dark color and the murmur of the crowd took a slightly bitter turn as word spread that the trader had undervalued the stone with intent. "Two thousand is all I can offer and still make my own slips when it reaches the border," he finally spit out, clearly concerned now. Traders that had a reputation for cheating were often cast out. They couldn't make a good living with the distrust they'd earned, and word spread quickly from village to village. Alador wondered if the trader would be forced to be generous the rest of the day.

Dorien turned to leave as if he didn't believe the man. Alador panicked, fearing that his brother had just lost him his slips and he'd have to wait an entire season before he could try to sell the stone again. Alador had never heard of anyone with two thousand slips – why couldn't Dorien just accept the offer? "I think we'll just find a mage who is need of a strong stone," Dorien said.

"All right – two thousand two hundred, but you are making it very hard to keep my own small ones fed," the trader countered, wringing his hands.

Dorien turned back around and dropped the stone down with a dull thud upon the weight board. "Done!" Dorien grinned, satisfied, as Alador stared on in amazement.

The trader went into his wagon and was gone for some time before a man emerged with him to help bring out a large chest. They lifted the chest up, and the makeshift table beside the weight board creaked with the weight of the box. The trader opened the lock and peeled back the lid, revealing strings of medure inside. The trader took out eight strings and pushed the chest toward Dorien. Medure had one hole in the end so that it could be strung; in large transactions, there were one hundred medure on a string. Alador stared at the box filled with string and slips of medure. Dorien closed the lid held out his hand for the key. Reluctantly, the trader handed that over as well, and Dorien locked it.

Alador had not yet said a word since the bartering began. Dorien nodded to Alador to grab a handle. Two thousand two hundred medure was going to weigh a fair amount, and – sure enough – it took both hands for Alador to carry his end. The crowd parted, the noise of their various conversations washing over him.

"…tried to cheat him…"

"…not fair that a mongrel gains so well!"

"…wonder if he wants small ones…"

Alador tried to block it all out as he and Dorien worked their way out of the trading circles. Twice they had to set the chest down so Aladoi could shake his hands out. Dorien just smiled at him. The blacksmith, of course, seemed unfazed by the weight of the box. Alador was still stunned. He couldn't believe a trader kept that many slips in his wagon. The heavily armed Daezun that traveled with the traders suddenly made sense.

When they finally stepped into the house, Alador's whole family was waiting. They gathered around while Dorien unlocked it again and opened the lid, and they stared at it in awe. Sofie reached out and caressed the medures in wonder. The box was full of the dull, hard metal, and the blue flecks sparkled in the lamplight. Alador picked up a heavy string himself and laid it on the table to stare at its beauty. No one spoke; the cooking fire and the clinking of the slips as Alador pulled them from the chest were the only sounds in the room.

Finally, his mother broke the silence as she looked up at Dorien. "How much?" she whispered.

"Two thousand, two hundred. The korpen dung tried to cheat the boy with five hundred." Dorien's contempt was obvious in his tone.

Alador finally found words. "How did you know he was…you know…under valuing the stone?" Dorien didn't mine bloodstones – he always said he preferred creating out of metal rather than finding it.

"He gave you the price far too fast, and he was licking his lips when he spit it out. I've seen stones half that size make five hundred."

"I never thought. I've always taken…" Alador sputtered. He flushed in embarrassment as he realized how many times he'd probably been shorted. He had never felt he had the right to argue with those older than himself.

Dorien laughed. "Never take a trader's first offer, Alador. They're trying to feed their own small ones and then some. They'll try to make as much as they can in a trade."

It made sense when one thought about it. Alador had just always been so grateful to have a slip that he never considered he might have earned more than one.

He could get fifty trading tokens for a single medure. Alador had always immediately traded in his slip for the trading tokens and been off to buy a sweetmeat or fletching, but most of his trading tokens went to his mother to help with his keep.

Alador slowly smiled. He took his knife out and cut the string of the one hundred slip circle he'd laid in front of him. "I've never been able to do much for naming days or anything," he said, referring to the days they celebrated their third turns. Many small ones didn't live past their second turn, so a small one didn't officially receive a name until they were three turns old. Alador had never been able to do the things he wanted for his siblings' naming days. "So today, we celebrate." He handed a slip to Sofie. "Spend it all on yourself." He smiled as she squealed with delight.

He turned to Tentret with two slips. "I know your drawing supplies are low." Tentret smiled slowly, uncharacteristically hugging his brother. Then he, too, rushed out. Alador reached into the box and took two strings and handed them to his brother. "I know you have your eye on Felia in Corsgrove as a housemate. Maybe now you can, you know, take on some small ones." His brother started to protest, but Alador held up the strings. "Call it a commission for more than five hundred slips."

Dorien smiled and took the strings. He disappeared after a moment, most likely to hide his strings – Alador could hear him banging about elsewhere in the house.

Strangely, Alador's mother hadn't said anything. There were no requests, no pointing out that she'd experienced the pain of birthing him. She was just staring at him in a strange awe. Alador shifted uncomfortably, not used to her silence. He reached in and pulled out two more strings. "I hope this will more than keep me till I find my own home and small ones to raise."

His mother took the strings slowly. "I knew...I knew it was right," she whispered

"Right? Right about what?" Alador looked at his mother with an arched brow.

"Choosing your father in the circle. I just knew it would turn out alright. I just knew it." Her eyes glistened with pride as she watched Alador.

"Maman, for long as I can remember, you've always thought that was a mistake." Alador looked at her in confusion. Had she lost her senses in the face of so many slips?

"'Cause no good seemed to be coming of it," she pointed out and grinned. "I am not a patient woman, child." Her large frame jiggled as she laughed.

Alador could not help but smile back; his mother had seriously understated herself. She had a hard time even waiting for water to boil, and Alador could recall her complaining at the pot in the fire on more occasions than he could count. Suddenly his mother hugged him. Her short, voluminous body pressed against him in a fierce embrace, making Alador groan in both surprise and embarrassment. Then, she also rushed deeper into the maze that was their home.

Alador was left alone with his box of medure. He stared at it, still in awe at the changes in his fortunes and even in his existence. He caressed the smooth metal and remained lost in his daze until Dorien came stomping back into the room.

"Now! Where to hide that box…" Dorien's booming voice made Alador jump. His startled wide-eyed expression brought a smile to Dorien's lips. "Sorry. I didn't mean to scare you. But we do need to put that box deep in the house and out of prying eyes." Dorien held up a chain and lock. "And we will be making sure it doesn't grow legs and wander off."

Alador grinned back at his brother. He pocketed a few slips and put the rest back into the box. They locked the box back up and then he and his brother lugged the box around until they finally found a good spot: the pantry off the kitchen. There was no external door, its contents were only pickling barrels and the like. Dorien and Alador hid the chest amongst the barrels, but not before Dorien chained it to the coal box for good measure. Once that was done, they both stood back to survey their work, satisfied that the chest was as safe as it could be made short of burying it somewhere.

Dorien ran a necklace chain through both the key heads and then placed it over Alador's head. "Even I am tempted. I suggest you always keep that close to your heart."

Alador stared at his brother, then spontaneously hugged him. Dorien just chuckled and smacked him on the back a couple of times before pushing him away. "I believe your friends are expecting to share in your fortunes, and trading will only be a bit longer before we have evening feast. Best run along now."

Alador nodded with a great smile. He also owed the bloodstone miners a night of drinking, but with the feast, he would wait to pay up that debt till after the traders left. His brother turned him toward the door and pushed him forward. Alador didn't need any more prompting to set out and find Mesiande, somewhere amongst the trading stalls.

Alador had never had as much fun as he had that night. It hadn't taken long to find Mesiande and Gregor. In fact, it was more likely *they'd* found *him*, given the ease.

The first stop had been at the stall for arrows, fletching and bows. Alador bought each of them new strings and searched through the feathers for the best fletching. His friends were stunned at the price and attempted to protest, but Alador would have none of it. If he couldn't have fun this one night, what was the point of even having slips?

They bought sweetmeats and looked at as many stalls as they could before the bell sounded. Slowly, the wagons closed up around them. It was interesting to watch: the traders seemed to finish their last sale in unison before beginning the process of packing up. The villagers slowly migrated to the feast as, one by one, the stalls became just wagons once more.

The feast was crowded, but food was to be had at every board. Each family had picked a board and filled it with their own offerings to the meal. Large platters of prang had been carved up and laid out on each table, and roasted fruit and nuts had been sprinkled around the meat. The smell of food filled the air and the shrieks of laughter, boisterous conversation, and cheerful music was a cascade of sound tumbling down around Alador. The good weather had held through the evening, and a warm breeze still filled the air as the sun settled behind the hills. People mingled and shared their offerings with friends, and even with people they didn't necessarily like. Animosity meant nothing during the feast.

The fire pit where the prang had been roasted was built up to light the circle, and dancing began as soon as the boards were cleared from the feast. Middlins and adults danced about in circles and pairs with no apparent rhyme or reason to their step. Small ones dashed about the dancers or attempted to imitate their elders, creating a vision that truly was the village. The Elders played flutes, drums or shakers. That was Alador's second favorite part – the pulsing beat of those drums seemed to reached deep into the souls of villagers and traders alike, and their feet couldn't help but keep time.

His favorite part, however, was watching Mesiande dance. In honor of the festivities, she had taken down her usual braids and her hair hung in waves that the long-standing braids had pressed into her hair. Despite its Daezun-brown color of her people, it glimmered in the firelight with streaks of golden fire. Mesiande closed her eyes as her feet kept rhythm to the drums, and she held her hands high while her fingers snapped to the same beat. She wore a skirt rather than her usual miner's garb.

To Alador, she was a picture of perfection. Her body, despite the days spent mining, seemed perfectly formed. She didn't have the over muscled appearance of many of the mining women. Only the palms of her hands gave any indication that she spent so many hours digging amongst stones. Alador smiled at her when she opened her eyes to see him watching. She waved him to her. He joined her, and the two of them stomped and spun to the pulsing music. The beat began to build in the song as the two of them moved about one another. Alador could feel the calluses of those small hands whenever Mesiande placed them against his to dance about in circles. As the music came to a sudden stop, she collapsed against him, laughing. She felt so right in his arms as he held her up.

As the evening progressed, he and Gregor both danced with Mesiande in turn. Sometimes the three danced together. Alador was leaner and a head taller than the other two, with strange eyes and fairer skin. But tonight, he did not feel out of place. Tonight, the village was home. As he watched Mesiande prance around in circles with Gregor, he smiled. Tonight, he would not have wished to be anywhere else.

Chapter Four

Village life did not tarry long, and despite the groans of those that had drunk far too much at the feast the previous evening, work began once more. It was planting season so there would not be any mining trips until the seeds were down. Alador was helping keep the korpen in front of the plows. The huge, lumbering beasts would see a piece of green, and wander off in search of a bite if not maintained firmly. They made the plowing easy enough but keeping them distracted from any tidbits could be a challenge. Alador had found it easier to manage the korpen by putting greens into his pockets. The beasts quickly figured out that if they followed him, Alador would slip them a bite now and then. The trick was to keep them placed, so the furrows were straight. It had been a wet spring, the ground was easily broken and plowed. The planting was a bit later this year as the village did not break the ground until the last of the snows melted off the surrounding hills. They had a particular hilltop they watched for an indication of when to start planting. It was usually pretty accurate for once the snow was off the top, usually the valley temperatures stayed warm enough for fragile new growth.

Alador's thoughts wandered as he strolled in front of the korpen leading them parallel to the last row. The mating ritual was still a ways off and yet still he wondered. He still had no idea what his role would be. He blushed at his own thoughts. Well, he knew if chosen what his role would be but what rituals or things were done before the circle dancing began is what he did not understand. It seemed unlikely that he would be chosen given his Lerdenian blood.

He looked up to see Mesiande a couple of rows over bent in planting. Her rounded form was even clearer to him in those tight mining pants. He shifted as his pants suddenly felt too tight, and looked away from her. Now if she would be in the circle, he would not be fearful. He knew that she would not hold his heritage against him. She was younger than he was, and he knew females did not join the circle until they could bear small ones. He glanced over to find her watching him, her hand over her eyes to shield them from the sun.

He turned his head as he heard her shout at him, his facing flushing at his thoughts as if she could read them. "You are going crooked!" Her voice was loud and had a tinge of laughter. The others villagers that were nearby planting looked up and frowned at him.

He looked down and immediately corrected the korpen. He had allowed them to wander out of the path while lost in his thoughts. He could hear her soft laughter and glanced back with a rueful grin. She shook her head and went back to planting once more. He was so absorbed with watching her that he did not hear Tentret approach. In fact, he was unaware of his presence until his brother slapped him up beside the head.

"She is too young." Tentret scolded firmly. Tentret did not speak much even in the walls of their home, but when he spoke it was usually with a purpose.

"She is not that much younger than me." Alador protested. He looked at his brother who was fairly close to him in age. Tentret was forty turns now and still seemed to have no interest in finding a housemate.

"Dorien should have never told you 'til it was time. You will get yourself banned before you even receive your training." Tentret eyed Alador with disapproval. He helped Alador pull up the plow and back the korpen up to where they had veered.

"Training? What training?" Alador asked. It had never occurred to him there was anything to train for those in the circle seemed so at ease unless it was their first year. "Does it not just happen sort of, well, naturally?"

"You do not think they send a male to the mating circle with no…experience do you?" Tentret shook his head. He was the one who spent a great deal of time in books and often helped teach the small ones their letters and other skills to do with writing and reading. He always expected everyone 'to just know' things unless they were small ones.

"I do not know. It is not like the men speak of it with the middlins." Alador flushed with color. However, middlins spoke of it often. By the time you had been into the center of the circle for drumming, you had looked a few times through the tent flap. It was also possible to hear the activities between songs. Alador had a fundamental concept of what was going on behind him.

"And now you know why, you are already losing your way at the thought of one you desire at the mention that you might be entering the circle." Tentret scolded. Tentret looked at Mesiande and back to Alador.

"So…what is this training?" Alador quickly tried to divert his brother. Perhaps Tentret would finally speak of the rituals that occurred prior.

"An elder will take you to her rugs and show you all that you need to know to insure not only pleasure, but a successful mating. The circle ensures we have small ones each season." Tentret offered.

Alador shuddered at the idea. "An Elder…" He squeaked. He immediately began picturing the eldest of the women, toothless and covered in folds of aging skin. "How can one even begin to…want…well you know."

Tentret laughed. "A man's nature is not that hard to coax forth, and they choose only those skilled for such tasks. Do not fret. This has been the way, and it has always brought success within the mating circle."

"I do not want to go to some elder's rugs." Alador complained his eyes moved to Mesiande and his blush deepening.

Tentret followed his gaze and frowned. "Do not get to set on that one, little brother. While she may choose to allow you to help raise her small ones, she is not likely to choose you in the circle with your mixed blood." Tentret grabbed hold of a korpen as they talked to insure that the animals kept the row straight.

"Mesi does not care about such things." Alador defended with a burst of unusual temper.

"Your Mesiande does not care in that she has chosen you as a friend. The matter might fall differently in the mating circle." Tentret cautioned. "She has Gregor as a friend as well, and she seems just as close with him."

Alador felt a strange rush of a feeling he did not understand. He looked over at Mesiande and found himself glaring at her. A strange sense of possessiveness swept over him forcibly. "She is mine." He snapped. "Gregor knows how I feel, he would not dare." Alador had never felt threatened by Gregor's presence in their friendship before, and did not understand the strange anger he felt at that thought. Truthfully, it was possible she would choose them both as she had when they danced, but at this moment, the idea made Alador boil inside.

Tentret sighed softly. "Alador, if any other heard such things from you, you would be fostered to a new village. Such demands are not allowed by a male. Mesiande will choose whom she mates with and whom her housemate will be. You will have no say in this matter. If you make a scene over it, the elders will send you out." Tentret spoke in a matter of fact manner.

There were few things that could get one fostered out and even fewer that could get one banished. However, fighting over one of the opposite sex was one of the few things that could get one sent to another village. Dorien had told Alador that due to the many dangers the Daezun faced, the elders did not allow dissension from within the village. It had been the way for as long as anyone could remember.

Alador quit speaking. He was clearly fuming as he walked. Tentret stared at him for a long moment. "I need to check on the other korpen." He walked off leaving Alador to keep the beasts moving. Alador did not look at Mesiande again for fear she would pick up on his thoughts. Tentret was right. He had seen a man sent away because he had become angered during the mating ritual. He had never come back, and the one he had desired had chosen another housemate. He had no doubt the elders would send him away despite his recent success in mining. Yet how could he stand by and watch as she took another into her arms, her rug, or even worse as her housemate. He remained dwelling on these strange new feelings as he plowed the rest of the day.

Alador finished his plowing as the sun fell behind the hill. He unharnessed the korpen and took them to the grazing fields. Gregor was just coming up with his korpen and Mesiande was with him. He saw their heads close together, and they were clearly sharing some amusement by the grin on both faces. He went the other direction, not ready to face either of them in his sour mood. Mesiande's faint call went unanswered as he crossed the grazing fields and hopped the fence.

He headed for a favorite spot down by the river. The river narrowed here through large rocks, and the spray left small cool pools where the winter flows had scoured divots in the rocks. The trees had long limbs that dangled over the water creating a cool, private copse. He sat watching the cascading swirls of rushing water, the sounds as soothing as the sight. He was still sitting there when Gregor found him. The sunlight behind the hill was now fading and it would be dark soon.

"There yah are." His friend plopped down beside him. Gregor had the same dull shade of brown hair and kept in the same shaggy fashion. He had a larger build and was shorter. The two were well matched for what Gregor had in size; Alador matched in speed. They had been friends since they had been sent to the elders' ring as small ones. Trelmar had been a bully even back then and Gregor had taken exception to him picking on Alador. Ever since, the two had been inseparable. "All right, Al, spill it out."

"It is something I cannot really talk about." Alador threw a rock into the river watching it disappear into the swirling depths.

"Let me take a guess. It is Mesi?" Gregor eyed Alador. He had always been able to read his friend, a fact that Alador often disliked. Alador's silence was confirmation enough for Gregor. "What she do this time?"

"She didn't do anything." Alador snapped. "It's me. Okay?" He wouldn't look at Gregor, and he could feel Gregor's eyes on him.

"No, I think it is me." Gregor said slowly. "Are yah jealous?" The expression on Alador's face when he asked was enough to confirm his suspicions. "Gods, Alador. I know yah like her. Yah have the slips. Yah and I both know she will choose yah."

"Not necessarily." Alador frowned at him. "You are pure Daezun, your blood is better for small ones. What if… what if that part matters to her?" Alador asked with both pain and anxiety.

"Now yah are being daft. It has never mattered to her before, why would it start now? Besides, I always thought it would kind of be...all three of us." Gregor teased, but his face sobered immediately when he saw Alador flush. "Umm, or not."

"I do not want to share her." The growl that erupted from Alador after that statement surprised Gregor and his eyes widened.

"Alador, yah got to get a grip on this before she enters the circle or yah will *never* be with her." Gregor's concern was evident in his tone. "Gods man, she is not even in the circle this year. Yah are being daft worrying about such things right now."

Gregor's words of caution were the second warning of the day, but despite the logic of both Tentret and Gregor, Alador found he did not care. He was not sharing her with anyone. However, one thing Gregor did say calmed Alador some. She was not in the circle this year, so he had no fear of her taking another to her bed. For now, all was safe. He took a deep breath and merely answered. "As usual, you are right."

Gregor smiled. It seemed as if his friend was always full of games and smiles. "Good. Now that this is settled," Gregor punched Alador lightly in the arm. "let's take a swim and wash off the day's work." Gregor hopped up and headed down stream where the cascade of rushing water swirled into a small natural pool, offset from the main river. The two of them used it as frequently as most Daezun preferred the hot house. It was also too deep for the small ones so only those that liked the cold water, and could swim, used it.

Alador watched him work his way down for a moment then sighed. Gregor was right. Nothing was going to happen this year. It was not either Gregor's or Mesiande's fault he was feeling this way. He was just being stupid. He pulled off his shirt as he followed Gregor down. Maybe the water would wash away his anger along with the day's sweat.

Chapter Five

Luthian stood at the balcony, overlooking the city, as the women that served him fluttered about behind him preparing a meal. He stood with a jeweled chalice watching the bustling activity. Silverport was laid out, as most cities of Lerdenia, in a series of tiers. The higher the tier, the higher one's standing in the circle of wizardry. It was not a matter of birth but a matter of skills in the magical arts. Each child was tested at a very young age and depending upon their skill, they were sent to the appropriate starting tier. Luthian was currently the Minister of Silverport. This title was voted upon by only those in the fifth tier, it was the highest tier.

Life in the high tier was pleasant. The halls were filled with luxuries from throughout the kingdom. Sometimes, a child of low skill was brought up to serve the high tier such as the women that now prepared his dinner. Later, he would choose among the women for one to warm his bed. He watched the setting sun with pleasure. The wind was such that the odors of the trench were not wafting up today. The trench was where those who had no magical skills and the outlanders lived and worked. Luthian had often dreamed of purging the trench but even he had to admit that the menial labors that those there provided were necessary for the rest of the city's beauty.

Luthian sipped his wine with a cold smile. His long graceful fingers grasped the jeweled chalice casually. It did not take one of intelligence long to learn how to survive in Silverport. Bloodstones could be purchased, and if one was lucky, magic gained from their murky depths. Rivals could be poisoned and removed from one's climb to a higher tier. Luthian has seen more than one mage removed from his path. He had been fortunate in that his innate skill had been with fire. This had started him in the third tier with more access than most. He had been able to use that skill to earn coin and purchase bloodstones. His climb had been slow and carefully plotted. He smiled remembering a time when he had shared the bed of one particularly influential fourth tier mage.

The man had been so enthralled with his new 'toy' that he had never seen the dagger coming. Luthian drifted off in thought to that moment when the corpulent mage had pulled him close, his fat lips wet with anticipation. As he had moved to claim Luthian's own, the knife that had found his heart had been swift. The man's shock had not been at the pain within his chest but the realization that a little third tier mage would bring a fourth tier mage to his knees. There had been no words between them as the man had slid to the floor. There had been no need. It was the way of the tiers. He still remembered the triumph of watching life fading from that locked, wordless gaze. Luthian's fingers tightened on the chalice. He started as a voice broke through his musings.

"Master Luthian, the stable lord has sent word and wishes to speak with you." His chamberlain called softly. He was cautious for interrupting the Minister could have deadly results. The man's tone was placating and gentle.

Luthian took a slow, calculating drink before turning to face the wizened man. "Near the dinner hour?" His eyes moved over the man, satisfied to see the shiver of fear that swept across the small man's body. "He had best have news of great import. See him to my office." Luthian turned back to finish watching the sunset. The stable lord was of the third tier and it would take some time for the word of permission and travel to bring the man to his door. There was no need to turn to see if his command was followed, Luthian was not denied.

Luthian gazed down at the fourth tier. The gleaming streets were laid with white bricks flickering with crystals. The rising stone towers spiraled about with the same stone. The name of the city came from this unique stone for when the sun was just so, the city turned to bright silver. It was blinding at the wrong angle to one looking up at the city as a whole from the plains. The tiers had developed both out of a need for social distinction and protection. During the war with the Daezun, it had quickly been learned that the upper tiers could be easily protected by making only narrow and arduous passages to them. There was a large white arching bridge from the plains to the third tier but a section of it was wood and could be dropped away to prevent an enemy from bypassing the trench, first and second tiers. It was a system that had insured Lerdenia had a firm hand in the wars.

On the opposite side of the city lay the vast port. The tall-masted ships were just visible from Luthian's vantage point. He had increased the size of the fleet since he had become minister. Too many times, he had felt that

the high circle did not take the threat of far off lands
seriously enough. In addition, trading with these lands
brought in goods that could not be produced with the
local craftsman. His free hand fingered the silk of his
robes. That material was one such item brought in by the
trading fleet. Luthian knew that the large ships were
impressive sailing into port and would give far off leaders
pause. If Lerdenian trading ships were so impressive,
what would their warships bring? Magic was innate in the
Lerdenian people, a fact that he had made sure was well
known in other ports.

Luthian roused from his musings and downed his
glass. He held it out without turning, and a young hand
took it from him. He turned from the balcony, his silken
robes flowing about a moment behind his body, the swish
of silk a warning to those close by. Women stilled and
eyes dropped as the Minister swept from the room. The
smell of food wafted to him as he passed. It would still be
there when he returned. In fact, if he took too long, it
would be replaced with fresh offerings before he ever
stepped into the room. Yes, life as the minister was quite
pleasant indeed.

Luthian did not pause as he entered the room
where his stable lord waited. The doors opened by two
armored and shorter men, their drab brown hair and
short statures giving way that they were of Daezun blood.
In comparison, despite his age, Luthian was tall and lithe.
His light blue robes flowed about him. They hid the drain
that the constant use of magic pulled from him. His hair,
a long straight length, was bleached white and he kept it
drawn back with a matching band of blue. His eyes
sparkled much like the streets, a soft lavender and silver.
Despite his lithe form, he was commanding in his
presence, and rare was it that all eyes did not move to him

when he entered. Despite the striking handsome face of the man, he was like marble, cold and hard, and his piercing eyes held no tenderness.

The stable lord, Veaneth, kneeled as he entered. "I bring news that I think will please you, Master Luthian." The man almost whined his words. His eyes staring at the Minister's shining black boots.

Luthian wrinkled his nose for the man often smelled of sour sweat, and his mewling was irritating. "That you are here at such an unseemly hour makes that quite clear Veaneth. Rise and speak your news." The minister's voice held the impatience of a man who did not wish to be kept from his dinner. Luthian moved to his desk and sat. He put his booted feet upon the rich wood and leaned back to eye the man. He watched as Veaneth struggled to his feet. The large man was winded from the climb required to cross from the third to the council tier. He held such weakness against the man.

Veaneth spoke somewhat breathlessly. "The decree to offer women of the first and second tier a higher path has brought forth many volunteers. Already three are confirmed with child." The man smiled. "It was verified this afternoon."

"These women understand that this pass to a higher tier will only occur if the child is born and shows the proper leanings?" Luthian was clearly pleased at this news. He knew that many of the council disapproved of his decree, but he had managed to sway enough votes to see it passed. He sat with his hands intertwined upon his chest.

"Yes Minister. I made them sign a contract so there could be no error including a clause of silence. They speak, and they will be sent to the trenches for life." Veaneth answered swiftly. He moved slightly closer to the desk. He kept his eyes trained upon the Minister's boots.

"We have twenty seven females and ten males. Needless to say, the ten males took some adjusting, but they are now quite pleased with their fate." Veaneth chuckled darkly.

"The Daezun women, their elixirs to prevent child should nearly have worn off, yes?" Luthian's question was with clear anticipation.

"Aye sir, I will have chambers prepared for those you care to breed personally." Veaneth looked at him hopefully. Since the two of them had started the breeding project, Luthian had not once let him take part. "Once the potion wears off, then they can be bred until it takes."

Luthian sat back doing some calculations. He had discovered during the war that some of the Daezun females who had been taken in battle had produced children with a unique quality. Daezun could not use magic. This made them ideal for digging bloodstones for they could not siphon the magics from the precious stones. Lerdenians' excelled at the use of such magics and their society was solely built around the ease and use of such skills. However, a Lerdenian was limited by his strength as to what skills he could pull upon and for a how long. These half breeds with a more Daezun build had been found to be able to use magics often needed in battle without the same drain upon their strengths...Some were deadly with a bow in ways that the average huntsmen envied. Others could manage elements tiring at a much slower rate than their Lerdenian counterparts. Luthian had gathered together those he had tested and found with the proper skills into an elite force that now served him. He had seen to their schooling personally, ensuring that only magics useful in battle were provided and doing much to insure their loyalty. The Black Guard currently only numbered slightly over a hundred, but he had plans to increase their numbers substantially over time.

Luthian also was staring at his boots as he considered the news and import. The Daezun should still be under Lerdenian rule for they were little better than beasts of burden. They had no skills in magic. Their choice of a simple village life when they could live in such higher luxury confused him. Why would anyone want to toil in the dirt if they did not have to so as to earn their keep? This desire to be a part of the land only confirmed they were little better than animals. However, he had to admit their skill in working as a reliable force had led to the Lerdenians being trapped in their cities under siege. The council had misjudged the Daezun seeing them as individual villages but somehow they came together as one in the second war. A treaty had been established. This treaty worked for now but was not in Luthian's long term plans. He had been but a boy when the war started and had made it only to the fourth tier when it had ended. No, this treaty did not fit into his plans at all.

Veaneth continued to stand and stare at the Minister's feet. Silence reigned heavy in the room, and Veaneth glanced higher to see if the Minister was even paying attention. Luthian's far off gaze seemed to cast through whatever he was looking at.

In truth, Luthian was seeing something beyond the stable lord. He had a larger vision. He intended to conquer the lands that the Daezun and the Lerdenians shared bringing it under a single rule. Then, he would turn his eyes to other lands. He would make Lerdenia an empire of such strength that all would bow in its path.

These sturdy half breeds would be his army. He was a patient man and the careful use of spells, potions, and magic's would insure Luthian had many years before him to see the matter completed. In addition to his program to breed the Daezun within the city with Lerdenians, he had the traders and traveling mages visiting mating circles and rituals as often as he could urge them into the Daezun lands. He had given those men potions and charms to insure they were often chosen in these circles. The resulting outcasts of half-blood were often rejected by their sturdier cousins. This suited Luthian well for he just swept in and cajoled the lost souls to his elite force. Daezun always made sure their small ones were well trained regardless of their origins. He had not been disappointed in this ploy.

"Then I am pleased with this news." Luthian suddenly announced. The stable lord started after such a long extended silence. Luthian reached into his desk as he placed his feet once more upon the floor. He tossed the man a small bloodstone.

Veaneth caught it deftly. It did not matter what power the stone held or if it would just bring a strengthening of his own limited skills. If he ever wanted to be more than the minister's boot licker, he had to have power. "Thank you Minister. I am but a servant to your pleasure." Veneto's platitudes were bordering on the whining of a child.

"See yourself out. My dinner waits." His lack of patience clear, Luthian rose gracefully and without a second glance left the room.

Veaneth watched him go, his face going hard. He knew that the minister would kill him as soon as look at him. Such was the way of the tiers, but he also knew that the project was frowned on by many of the council. As such, Luthian needed him and his silence. He turned on his heel, no longer the groveling servant and strode from the room. Outside of Luthian's presence he was treated well, for everyone knew that for some reason Veaneth held favor.

Luthian returned to his well laid dinner. His meal was, as he expected, warm and waiting. Four woman stood in attendance about the table. As soon as he was seated, one moved to him and cleaned each of his hands with a warm wet towel. Her eyes never touching the man's face. Her beauty was enhanced by the scant robe that hid little of her breasts from his gaze. Luthian, however, did not even seem to notice. Lost in his thoughts of power and conquest, such beauty at his beck and call was his expectation. As soon as he was washed, the women moved soundless about Luthian to serve him and to insure his plate and glass were kept full.

Luthian did not speak during his dinners alone. He used this time to consider the events of the day and how they fit into his overall plans. He was irritated that his meal had been interrupted yet again by news that the bloodstone trader had arrivd. He has sent news the man could await his pleasure. He finished his dinner lost in his thoughts and plans.

As his plate was being removed, a young woman, new to his service, bumped his arm as he sipped his wine. His wine splashed slightly upon his robes, and his surprise brought his eyes upon the girl. She stood before him trembling. Her young body was tense as she stood unspeaking before the minister. No one moved as they waited to see what this sacrilege would bring to the woman who stood before Luthian.

"You made me spill my drink." He commented quietly, his voice was as liquid as the silk he wore.

"Yes Master, I am so sorry. I did not mean to touch your arm." The girl's voice was barely audible. She was biting her lip as she stared at the floor.

Luthian tipped her face up to look at him. His cold white fingers were in stark contrast to her warm rich skin. He realized her eyes were like emeralds, and he liked the fear that shimmered in their depths. "You are new?" He was forced to ask as he often did not pay attention to those that attended his meals. However, now that she had gained his attention, he found her features pleasing and as his eyes roved over her body, a stirring of interest.

"Yes Master." She whispered. Her voice warbled in tone as she cast about to the other women as if seeking help.

Luthian could feel her terror growing as he held her chin to force her face to gaze once more upon his own. Even so, her eyes did not quite meet his. "You know that to spill upon the Minister is unforgivable in service?" His soft question was deadly.

"Y-yes Master." The girl's eyes filled with tears.

He smiled almost feeding on the terror that was palpable beneath his fingers. "What is your name?" He asked slowly setting down his wine glass. While fear was not new to his experiences with women, it was clear that this woman did not know quite what it was she had to fear. The unknown was such an exquisite fear to behold.

"Keelee." She answered, her eyes following that wine glass. She still stood holding his plate. She was shaking so hard that the fork rattled upon its fragile surface.

"Well then, Keelee, it is fortunate that I am in a fair mood. You may make it up to me in my bed this night. I suggest you do not disappointment there. I would hate for this to be your first *and* last day at my table." He drawled out slowly letting his fingers fall away from her chin.

The fascinating eyes were obscured by the curtain of deep brown hair kept loose as he commanded by those that served him. He heard her mutter, "Yes Master." She turned and fled his presence. He chuckled softly. He picked up his glass and downed the last. Tonight would be most pleasing.

Finished with his dinner, he rose from the table and moved to the receiving hall. He had received word that a load of stones were in and that there was one of an unusual color and size. He had been irritated that his dinner had been interrupted once more and in uncertain terms made it clear that the trader could wait. The chamberlain had been forced to go and change his scorched robes.

As the Minister walked into the room, the irritating Daezun trader began bobbing and bowing. "I have brought you a fine batch from down south, Minister. You will be most impressed." He led the minister to the table where various stones were laid out. The table had been covered with a black cloth to set the stones to their best advantage. The trader, as always, had arrayed the stones from the smallest to the largest.

Luthian had arranged for many of the central traders to give him first pick of the stones. Many were the usual small stones of a trade. The problem with small stones was that one did not know if it were a unique power or just a surge to strengthen what one already had. He worked his way to where the larger stones were laid out. He chose several stones to have set aside. He did not quibble or barter. The man knew to charge him a fair price.

"I heard a tale you have found one of an incredible size, but I see nothing unusual." Luthian eyed the man. If such a stone existed, it had better be here.

The trade smiled with delight. "Aye, Minister. I have kept it special for I knew you would want it." The man pulled a small wooden chest from under the table and set it down proudly.

Luthian eyed the chest. If the chest was any indicator of size, then the stone would be bigger than any he had ever seen. Such a stone would have the main power of whatever dragon formed it. He licked his lips in anticipation for there had only been one other stone known to contain such power and it had been many centuries ago. "Well, open it." Luthian demanded. He clasped his hands behind him to prevent himself from just ripping the chest open himself.

The trader unlocked the chest in excitement for with this find; he would not have to go out in the winter seasons. He would be able to stay home with his small ones and housemate. He uncovered the pure glass stone with a flourish and stepped back for he had seen the desire on the minister's face. Yet instead of the pleasure and anticipation he had expected, he saw fury. The trader's eyes flew open with alarm.

"Do you think me a fool?" Hissed Luthian as he turned around to fully face the trader. "Who did you sell its magics too?" Luthian tone was ominous, and his hands began to glow an eerie yellow.

The trader stepped back as if that fury was palpable. "N-no one s-sir. It...It was like that when I bought it. I...I did not think it would hurt the value. I swear. It has been locked within since I purchased it." The trader squeaked, dropping to his knees in fear. He had never seen the Minister angry, but he had heard the tales of those that had crossed him. He had never heard of any leaving such ire unscathed. The pulse of the trader's rapid heartbeat was visible in his neck.

"Bought it where? What other mages were present?" He demanded of the groveling man. He slowly circled the man upon the ground much as a wolf circles his injured prey.

"S...Smallbrook m...my lord. The Daezun village of Smallbrook and there weren't no mages there." He put his face to the floor in hopes of appeasing the Minister. "I...it was a fair stone, and I will give it to you. I won't want nothing of it." He offered in a panic. His voice muffled against the floor.

"You fool!" Shouted Luthian. "Are you really so stupid?" The sneering loud tone brought a visible wince from the trader upon the floor. "It is clear because its magic has been given. What miner sold the stone? I want a name!" Luthian kicked the trader over, the audible crack of a rib resounded in the room. "A name." He demanded. Luthian's tone suddenly softer, cold, and definitely vicious. Luthian's hand crackled with the power of the fire he could wield.

"Alador...it was a man named Alador. Still a middlin and didn't even know what he had. I swear it." The man was practically sobbing now for even he could feel the power radiating from the Minister though he dared not look.

Luthian paused, his foot now on the Trader's chest who lay beneath him on the floor. . Smallbrook...Alador...Alador...why did he know that name? Then it dawned on him. That was one of his brother's spawn from the project. The boy had come into his power. By blood, he had come into power with that stone? He looked back at the chest with alarm.

He removed his foot off the trader and moved to the chest gazing down at its contents. The empty stone was beautiful but powerless. Who knew how much power the boy had absorbed? Did the boy even know how to use it? It was not good that such power was uncontrolled. However, one benefit of the treaty included a clause that if any of Lerdenian blood and magical skill were found on Daezun lands, the Council had the right to demand they be turned over for training. This had suited the Daezun well for they distrusted magic.

His anger cooled some as he stared at the stone in calculation. The whimpering of the trader still lying where he had left him interrupted Luthian's thoughts. He cursed softly and with a fluid motion turned and released the spell at the groveling man. He did not even stay to see if the trader lived beneath the column of fire that had risen up from his writhing form, the music of his screams pleasing enough. At the door, he paused to look at the guard. "Clean it up and put all the bloodstones in the vault." He did not acknowledge the guard's chest salute. Such response was expected. Besides, he had more important things on his mind.

He strode down the empty hall in anger and frustration. So much power that had been so nearly his and his nephew had it. His half-breed, tierless nephew who probably didn't even know what gift had been given him. The stark white halls resounded with the steps of his boots as he strode in anger. "Get me my brother...Now!" He bellowed. The words echoed down the vast empty hall. He didn't care who heard. He didn't care who acted. He knew someone would see it done. If he couldn't have the power, then he would control the boy!

Chapter Six

Life started to gain some typical routine to it. There were subtle differences now. People would wave to him as he moved through the village and more of the middlins had invited him hunting or fishing. It was the welcome that he had always craved, and though it sometimes felt odd, it also was uplifting. Work in the village was never truly done, so the sign that one could sneak off for more enjoyable things was when the sun began its drop behind the hill. Though the direct sun was gone, it remained light for a while longer leaving plenty of time for fishing or a swim.

He had taken to sneaking off to practice more so he could explore this new found ability to focus on a target and have it seemingly loom before him. Every time he concentrated, the target would jump towards him, it was unsettling and would sometimes slow his shot. He knew in battle that he could not be distracted by the target's sudden close appearance. Besides, practicing usually took his mind off the strange feelings of possessiveness he had been having whenever he thought of Mesiande.

His thoughts wandered back to Mesiande. He had always seen her as his best friend. He had occasionally wished for more. It was another reason he had taken to practicing, he was concerned about his changes in feelings. He was so lost in these thoughts and the repeated twang of the bow releasing arrows that for a moment, he did not hear the alarm bells. The alarm bell had not been tolled since the end of the war. He, himself, had never even heard it, though he knew what it was immediately. Small ones were trained to the alarm's rhythm with a handheld bell. He glanced about quickly for some seen threat but could find nothing. His eyes focused in on the small ones playing down at the river. Two elders were trying to gather them up and herd them towards the safety of the village. However, there were several small ones, and though the older ones were helping, it was clear that this group would be in danger if the threat was real. A growl erupted from his throat. He had to protect the fledglings. The intensity of that thought, of fledglings rather than small ones, washed over him with great drive. He broke into a run and headed for the group.

As he reached the cluster of small ones, the threat came flapping into view. He stood for a long, stunned moment. A dragon spiraled lazily, its red scales gleaming in the sunlight. He had dug the bones of dragons for so long that he had forgotten from where they came. The dragon was magnificent. He watched with amazement as it moved. It was more impressive in person than the red dragon of his dreams, though it bore a striking resemblance. Its large massive wing thrusts gave it the appearance of little effort to remain aloft. The wings seem to snap with each downward thrust.

Dragons usually left villages alone. There was enough food for all in the wilds, therefore, they did not have to ravage the villages for food. However, it was not unheard of for a dragon to hit a caravan carrying precious goods. He had seen a dragon a time or two in the distance but never one this close. They could be seen carrying off a prang now and then. He had once seen one from a great distance rise with a korpen in its grasp and drop it to crack its hard shell. It had been too far away to go and watch to see if this tactic had worked for the dragon or not.

He watched the dragon fly around as if it were looking for something. Behind him, the elders gathered up small ones. "Do not take them to the village. The dragon's intent is not known, and it is clear he is circling it." Alador commanded them as if he were in charge. It did not occur to him he was ordering elders. Apparently it did not occur to the elders either for they huddled the children together and ceased trying to herd them to the village.

The dragon had not yet made a threatening move. Alador could see from his position that the villagers had taken defensive positions on the roofs of various houses. Bows were at the ready, but no one fired. Dragons were respected amongst the Daezun, so unless the dragon acted aggressively, the people would not fire. Alador could not recall any visits to Smallbrook by dragons, but there were tales that they could speak. Recently, the tales were more that the dragons had forgotten the Daezun, and had taken to robbing from them.

The elders managed to move the children into the bushes. The small ones were used to playing hide and seek amongst these high bushes, and many had small hollows from years of the play and fort making. Alador's eyes had not left the dragon. His heart was racing as he also feathered his bow, keeping it lowered and watchful. The dragon had banked, its back was towards Alador. He was so close that Alador could clearly see the varying reds of the scales. Two great horns laid back almost against his head, starkly black against the fiery red scales. The nose of the dragon had appeared soot-covered before it had turned away. A black stripe continued from the head down a ridge of spikes that traveled down the dragon's spine, contrasting sharply. It had a long tail ending in a mace like shape with spikes standing rigidly out in all directions and some of the spikes appeared broken. Its tail rippled in movement with its wings much like a snake moving along the ground. Its wingspan was enormous and even as it banked away from him, he could almost feel the power of their mighty thrust. He recognized the main bone of the wing for he liked to find wings for his mining. A large spear like horn protruded from the front of that massive wing bone. Alador was sure that on the ground with those spears and that tail, this dragon was as formidable as it would be in the air. He whispered a silent plea to the gods that it would find nothing of interest and move on.

As if in defiance of his prayer, he watched with alarm as the dragon pulled in a great breath. It banked sharply and sailed right over the village, fire shooting from its massive maw. The rush of flame from the dragon's mouth caused Alador's mouth to open in surprise. He had heard that the dragons could breathe out weapons like fire, each color with a differing breath, but he had never seen it. The dragon sailed over an outer row of houses. Alador was close enough to hear the blazing breath rain down upon the roofs of the thatched huts. A flurry of arrows were released by those upon the rooftops.

Small ones screamed behind him drawing the attention of the dragon, its large head swiveling towards the sound. Alador stood upon a small rise before the sage bushes that protected the small ones from the dragon's view. It was as if everything slowed down before him. He could hear his heart beating loudly. He could hear the elders attempting to silence the children. He could feel the dragon's great lavender eye upon him. The gaze of the dragon and Alador seemed to lock as the dragon's head jumped towards him much as the targets did. His breath caught as something seemed to hit him in the stomach. The arrows that had hit the massive serpent seemed to fall away, and he could see none that had landed any harm although a few had stuck where scales met.

The dragon banked sharply and headed straight for Alador. He stood staring for he was sure there had been recognition in that dragon's eye. There was no doubt in Alador's mind. This was the red dragon he had seen in his dreams, the one called Keensight. He was so mesmerized by the dragon that he almost did not realize it was bearing down upon him. He snapped out of the haze he was in at just the last moment, diving to the ground as claws the size of spears grasped for where he had stood only moments before. The wind of the dragon's passing whipped the weeds and brush about him. He rolled up to his feet at the sound of the small ones crying. Meanwhile, the dragon slowly banked back around.

"You must protect the fledglings. A dragon is most vulnerable when it draws breath to bring forth its weapon."

The deep, commanding voice resonated through him. It felt right and powerful and his eyes narrowed as they sought Keensight's form.

It finished banking around and was coming back towards him. He feathered another arrow and drew the bow back taught. He concentrated and as had been happening lately, the face of the dragon seemed to enlarge before him. He could see the wafts of smoke drifting from its nostrils. Its massive head was filled with small spikes covered in soot. He had never actually seen a dragon up close. The dragon opened its giant maw to draw breath. The teeth were as sharp as the glass knives of the ice caverns. There, the pale pink of the throat was visible as it breathed in. He let his arrow fly and watches as it sank deep into the back of the dragon's throat. The dragon screamed in pain and agony, its wings shifting position as it attempted to stop its descent to move away from the pain. Its frantic flapping whipped him with the wind caused by the force of their vertical thrusts. The dragon's guttural screams pierced the air and making him cringe against the intensity.

Having already drawn its breath for fire, the great serpent shot the fire up into the sky, the flames erupting forth like a volcano spewing its molten contents. Based on the frantic flapping and clawing at its face, it had left the arrowhead lodged in its throat. The dragon screamed in fury, its tail whipping widely. It clawed at its mouth with its front feet, its wings flapping just as madly. Eventually it turned and flapped away, Alador had feathered another arrow and kept it trained on the beast till it floundered over a rise. He dropped to his knees, his heart racing and his legs trembling too hard to hold him.

For a moment, it seemed as if the dragon had been looking at him specifically and not the children. He had felt recognition between them. Not only that this was the dragon in his dreams, but the dragon had seemed to know him as well. It had left off its attack on the village to turn to him. His first thought had been that it was after the small ones, but it had made no attempt to turn back to the children. That second pass had been as if it came for him. How had he known to shoot into its mouth? He tried to remember being taught this weakness in dragons, but he could remember no such lesson. He was sure that the voice was not his own memory. He slowly let the bow string relax as his thoughts raced.

Maredeth, the elder closest to him, stood staring at him. The small ones, however, erupted from the brush with excitement and cheering. They all seemed to be touching him at once. The babble of their voices filling the air.

"You got him." "You saved us." "Did you see that shot." "I bet Trelmar could not made that shot." "I can't wait to tell maman." "Look! The village is on fire."

The last uttered sentence drew Alador's eyes. Mesiande had been in the village. He grabbed his bow and jumped to his feet. Smoke billowed from the village. Many of the middle and inner circle houses were close together. A fire started from the top would be devastating. There were cries of pain and screaming still coming from the village. He could hear elders shouting orders for water. "We have to help!" He shouted to the elders behind him.

He took off at a dead run. He hit the outer ring leaving the small ones far behind. Frantically he looked about for Mesiande as he ran towards the area of smoke. Many houses were on fire, and the entire village was forming a bucket line. He still didn't see her. He looked about in panic. He ran to her house, it was not on fire. He hollered within, but no one was there. He knew she would be helping, so he headed toward the area that was blazing. Twice he had grabbed ahold of women that looked like Mesi from behind, only to realize they were not her. He did not take the time to do more then utter a swift apology before hurrying forward. Finally, with great relief, he saw her near the end by one of the wells. He joined the line, and soon was helping pass water buckets as fast as they could be pulled from the well. He made sure he was positioned with his back to hers. She was passing empty buckets back towards the well.

It took the village nearly three hours to put the fires out. They had spread fast as most of the upper structures of the houses were made of wood. The bottom floor was made of stone to help prevent fires caused by cooking. Fire did not usually rain down from above. The council quickly organized the efforts, moving people to surround the fires and work inward. This prevented the fire from spreading to untouched buildings.

It seemed to take forever. As fast as a bucket could be filled, it was swiftly passed down the line. A second line returned them keeping the buckets moving. Other villagers used large wet blankets to try to smother flames.

When at last the fires were out, most of the villagers were exhausted. Many were blackened by soot. The village was called to the center circle and wearily the injured and exhausted were helped the center. Healers moved about tending burns and any injuries. They moved as if their limbs were made of lead. Even the children clustered in quiet groups. Now that the fires were out, the shock of what had occurred was setting in.

Word spread quickly that six had died in the direct blast of the dragon, caught upon or in their homes, they had been unable to escape the flames in time. The sound of their housekin mourning could be heard at the far edge of the circle. The village had not lost so many at once since the wars. The grief and shock was palpable. The Daezun revered the dragons, so to have one attack with such unprovoked rage left many in disbelief.

Alador moved to Mesiande and put an arm around her to comfort her for she stood in dazed shock. "You okay?" He asked softly in her ear.

She nodded yes and looked up at him with tear filled eyes. At that moment, his brave little friend looked small and helpless. He reached out and tenderly wiped a soot filled tear that trailed down her cheek. She laid her face into his hand and then just walked into his arms. He held her tenderly as she stood shivering in his arms. It felt right, to hold her this way.

The elders stood in the center of the circle conversing. Other than the sobs of those who had lost kin, there was only the softest murmurs of conversation. The people were tired and confused. Alador was so busy comforting Mesiande that he did not see Maredeth point to him. It wasn't till the village was suddenly silent that he looked up and saw all eyes on him. He flushed and looked down at the intimate comfort he was giving to the middlin in his arms. Alador stood uncomfortably, unsure if he should push her away or what he was to do.

"Alador, come forward." Velkar called. He was the leader of the elders' council.

Alador blinked a few times and slowly let go of Mesiande. She looked up at him with concern and confusion. Alador, himself, looked about him worriedly. What had he done now? Certainly he was not to be scolded for giving his friend comfort? He moved slowly to stand before Velkar.

"Meradeth tells me that you sent an arrow into the mouth of the beast, and this is why the small ones were not burned by its breath. Is this so?" Velkar's voice held an authority that few ignored. Despite his age, he still carried himself with a strong air of confidence. His eyes were sharp, and his presence was commanding. Alador noticed him when he entered a room even if he never spoke.

"Yes Elder." Alador answered quietly. "It was naught but a lucky shot is all." He breathed out with relief, thankful that he was not in trouble for holding Mesiande.

"Luck seems to follow you these days Alador. This village is beholden to you for we would have lost far more. It has been decided by the council that Alador of the house of Alanis will join the circle of men this night." Velkar held up a hand as a murmur went around the circle. "A planning council will be held tomorrow and you will join us there." Middlins were not allowed in council so it was clear this sudden move up of his ritual was to avoid breaking rules.

Alador sighed softly. He was going to find himself on the outside again as such recognition was not normal in the village. He would rather they bend their ways for once and just let him report to the council as a middlin. That was the only thing he found he did not like about his people. They were rigid in their adherence to rituals and rules. Henrick, Alador's father, had told him in Lerdenia, laws adjusted as times changed. Henrick had gone on to emphasize that the Daezun did not change. The eyes of the village today held no judgment. He saw many nod in agreement with the elder as he looked around.

As he looked about the circle, his eyes met Trelmar's. There, he did not see acceptance. With Trelmar, it appeared that nothing had changed. That was not quite correct, he realized that it was hatred that seethed in the middlin's eyes as the two's vision connected for a long moment. Alador realized in that moment, he was no longer a mere victim of mischief. He had made an enemy.

Alador started when the chief elder began speaking again and snapped his attention back to Velkar. "Dorien, see your brother bathed and readied for the ritual. I will see to it that arrangements are made in the ceremonial hut."

Dorien stepped up and nodded. "I will see him prepared Elder." Dorien took the stunned middlin by the arm and began to lead him through the people. Everyone seemed to want to touch him as he went by. It was an odd sensation of so many hands passing over him as Dorien led him away from the circle. Alador said nothing. He turned his head back and looked at Mesiande. She was biting her lip and looking concerned as Dorien pulled him off.

Chapter Seven

Luthian had not been able to sit still, and so he paced back and forth, his hands clasped behind his back. His thoughts were on the size of that bloodstone and the sheer power it had held. Did the boy even know what he possessed? Had he found some rogue mage to instruct him? Was he as malleable as most outcasts of the Daezun? He must still be within the village ranks if he was mining and trading. It would make him not yet an adult. How old was that boy? His brother had told him in one of his long ramblings about his trips, but he could not remember. It had not really mattered to him much about what his brother spawned as long as those with some capacity for magics were brought into his elite force.

He continued to pace back and forth in his study. It was immaculately maintained, and the library was the most extensive in all of Silverport. Luthian had added every book he could find on magic. He had a collection of maps and tales of the known world beyond the isle. Every mage he had removed from his path had been brought down by the knowledge in Luthian's library and then in the mages' demise, he had pilfered to add to its voluminous shelves. It smelled heavily of old leather, a hint of dusty parchment and the rich sweet smell of a good tobacco. The floor was a black marble that was shined daily by the servants until it was almost mirror like. It was set off by rich warm thick carpets mulled in a deep red wine color. It spoke of slips, luxury, and power. It was the perfect backdrop for his meetings, for Luthian was as well maintained as his surroundings.

When Luthian had originally sent for his brother, Henrick, he had not been in the city. It turned out that he had been out on one of the routes assigned to him by the council. Luthian had been forced to wait three weeks for his brother's return. He had received word that Henrick had returned to the city last evening. He had forced himself to be patient, and had not sent for him till a couple of hours ago. Patience was not Luthian's virtue. He had forced his energy into bedding many of the Daezun women. There had been a certain pleasure in seeing them beneath him without the protection of their precious potion. Their fear had been almost intoxicating. He smiled at the memory before current matters wormed their way back into his thoughts once more.

Where was his brother? He was in the fifth tier and so had access to the council's tier. He should have been here by now. Luthian's brow was furrowed, and his eyes were narrow slits. His pace was hard, and his boots could be heard tapping out upon the marble floor. The Black Guards assigned to him had been wise enough to step out and guard his door outside the room. He was furious. Furious he had not paid attention. Furious that a stone of such power and slipped his grasp, and furious that his brother had not found the boy's capabilities sooner. This was made worse by the fact that his brother was keeping him waiting. People did not keep Luthian waiting. His anger rose as he considered the many things he could do to the impertinent. A malicious smile slowly formed on his face before he shook his head to focus back to the problem at hand.

Henrick had two sons from his excursions into the Daezun lands. Luthian's thoughts turned to the Daezun. The two cultures were at peace, but for the most part, neither had much use for the other outside of the trade that took place. The bloodstones could not be harvested by any of Lerdenian blood for the magic was always seeped from it, and while some protections could be found, most of those seeking the stones wanted the power for themselves. The Daezun were a hardier folk and more suited for such work and had the added benefit that they could not harvest the stones for their own use. The Daezun tolerated the healers and enchanters of Lerdenia because they could not use magics and some things only a mage healer could cure or fix. All healers that used magics had at least some Lerdenian bloodline. In truth, the two people needed each other, but Luthian would prefer it under his rule.

More intense healings were the most frequent of Daezun requests. Enchantments to bring forth better stock and crops were also another important aspect of this trade off. It had been part of the terms of the peace treaty; trade of bloodstones for magics and items needed in a daily village life. Luthian held them in contempt. They seemed to have no use for the finer things in life like wine or silk. They were led by their elders, and most of those in power were women. Women ran their households and had an equal voice in their council of elders. Women had no place in leadership unless they held great power and definitely should not lead the home. He preferred them beneath him in his bed or silent in their service. They should serve the men in their lives, but this was not the Daezun way. The Daezun way, he scoffed aloud, they were little better than animals with no refinement.

Henrick had too much fondness for his trips into the Daezun lands. It was one more reason Luthian held his younger brother in such contempt. He did not know how his brother could handle these overbearing, independent females. Luthian made sure all those in his stable were properly cowed before they were ever considered for breeding mares. If they had a tongue on them or a will that seemed unbreakable, he used them before the others as examples. More than one willful bitch had been left smoldering upon the floor, a visual example to others that would dare defy his commands. To him, they were a lesser people, a necessary blight upon the edges of the Lerdenian rule. If they were not fit for his Black Guard, then they should be slaves to the mage council's whims. His lip curled with the strength of his contempt.

Luthian walked to his desk and surveyed the island map. The Daezun currently held one third of the great isle. Despite having magic, Lerdenia had been unable to uproot the Daezun during the Great War. They had a way of melding into the landscape about them. They had made warrens like vermin, far beneath the ground where they could go undetected. Divining mages were few and far between as this was a magic not often used or even discovered in the bloodstones. When the Lerdenian council would find such a mage and bring them into battle, the Daezun archers seemed to have a knack for somehow seeking them out. One of the Black Guard had told him recently that he could feel such a mage when they were searching the fields of magic. Luthian traced the line on the great map before him. Lerdenia should own all the Great Isle and the Daezun should be nothing but slaves to Lerdenia's pleasure. His eyes narrowed, and despite being alone, he snarled at the idea. Yet the Daezun had managed to hold their ground over the many centuries of conflict. It was not until Lerdenia realized that no new magics were coming forth that they had even considered peace. Luthian planned to bring an end to the time of peace and make it a time of rule. But to do that, he had to be able to fight Daezun on their own ground.

That had been the start of creating and molding the Black Guard. He had named them for the black leather and mail armor they wore. He saw them as slightly above the Daezun people because at least they could be taught the battle magics. Due to being raised in Lerdenian luxury or cast out of their own Daezun homes, Luthian had been able to spoil them just enough to keep their attention. His harsh expectations enforced by corporal punishments, often lethal, commanded a feared regard. He had no qualms at killing one for a failure to study. Of course, he made sure it was through an exhibition of his own fiery power, and only to ones who had failed to live up to the potential that they had initially shown. Luthian did not care whether the Black Guard respected him, feared him, or saw him as a benefactor as long as they followed his orders. His mind drifted to the young female that had failed to practice her archery skills and who had not lived up to his expectations. He had shown the Daezun not only how to treat a lesser female but also what happened when they failed him. He could still hear her screams from within the fiery column he had called down upon her when he had finished.

The door swung open, its hinges creaking from the heavy metal weight, startling the mage from his thoughts. Luthian spun around. His brother was so unlike him. He wore black robes trimmed in silver. His hair was still jet black, and his eyes seemed to glisten with an intelligence that made Luthian nervous. Yet his brother never overstepped his place. He seemed to have no designs for anything higher than the fifth tier. This suited Luthian for he suspected there were depths to his brother that he did not understand. His brother had always seemed weak at first, and so he had sent him out as one of the traveling enchanters and healers. He had given him the charms to insure chances into the circles. However, on a trip a couple years ago, Henrick had come back different and that difference had made Luthian wary. He was sure his brother had laid hands on a more powerful stone, but when he had attempted to press the issue, his brother had seemed as simple as ever. Henrick had become more independent and free with his thoughts. The usual boot kissing behaviors had ceased. He smiled absently. He had rather liked instilling those behaviors in his brother, maybe he needed to do it again.

Henrick sauntered into the room. His voice was hoarse and raspy. "Sorry brother, I have been ill. I fear I had to dress to attend your summons. How may I serve?" He bowed low before Luthian.

Luthian's eyes narrowed for his brother was rarely sick. However, he did indeed look pale and somewhat harried. His robes were wrinkled and appeared to have been slept in. That was another difference he had noticed over the last two years, Henrick had become much more fastidious about his appearance. This unkempt state was not his usual manner in the last two years. Luthian shook himself from his thoughts. "The son you have in Smallbrook, when did you last test him?"

Henrick looked at his brother slightly in surprise. "I am due to test him in the next trip. Why do you ask?

You seemed to have no interest in the boy in our previous conversations." Henrick's usual bored expression of late was broken as his eyes moved to Luthian.

"He has come into his power, you fool. You missed it, and he has harvested from a rather large stone." Luthian snarled out in tones that were harsh with his displeasure. His sharp eyes were intent upon the lesser mage.

"Oh, how did you get this news?" His tone casual and drawn out, Henrick dropped into a leather chair by the fire putting his feet up on the small table before him, his back to his brother. His continued tone seemed to indicate that the younger mage was aware. "Forgive me but I am still taxed from my illness." Henrick's manner was almost as if he were being inconvenienced, his manner casual as he plucked at a thread upon his sleeve.

"A trader attempted to sell me an emptied stone and gave the name of the one who harvested it as one Alador of Smallbrook. I doubt there are two." Luthian frowned with displeasure at his brother's lack of respect to his position. He moved about where he could see his brother's face, but the man was just staring into the flames. Had his brother known? Luthian watched him. "You need to bring him to me." Luthian commanded. Luthian turned sharp and stomped back to his desk, his tone was such that this should have been the end of the conversation, so he was a bit startled when Henrick softly spoke.

"Is that wise brother? Perhaps we should just kill him. Certainly an untrained Daezun with such power would be a concern for you," Henrick casually stated, not looking up from the fire. His finger still toyed with the loose thread of his robe.

Luthian blinked in surprise. Ever since the boy had been found to be Henrick's, the man had seemed proud of his spawn and protective. What had brought about this change of heart? Luthian had expected Henrick to rise with excitement to bring in the beloved son he had once rained praises on after every trip. "This would be correct except in this case there is an advantage to his control." Luthian picked up a chalice from his desk and walked towards the fire. He sipped at it as he stood to the side. His eyes never left off staring at the side of Henrick's head.

Henrick looked up at him. "Oh, what would that be?" Henrick quit playing with the thread and rubbed his throat absently.

Luthian smiled coldly, and he drew out the words. "He is family." He could not wait to get his hands on that power. It was too bad that you couldn't kill another mage and steal their power in their death. He would much rather kill his competition than a dragon. Luthian's greed and malice was not hidden with that thought.

Henrick gazed at his brother for a very long time. The silence hung between them. "What if you cannot control him?" The soft question hung in the air between them.

Luthian took another sip before he answered. "Then we kill him, but let us try to find the extent of his power and attempt to bring it under our command." Luthian's calculating mind was still considered the possible powers and uses of such a Daezun half breed. He did not consider a halfblooded Black Guard a threat. He also did not intend for there to be an "our command" but for now this would appease his brother.

"Do you wish me to make my usual trip or go straight there?" Henrick asked with a slight frown.

Henrick clearly looked displeased at the idea of setting out. "The ball, after all, is this week. I have a set of new robes on order. It would be a shame to waste them." Henrick's drawl indicated he really had no desire to be upon the road any time soon.

Luthian rolled his eyes. Typical of his brother to care more about his appearance at some gossip filled mongering event than the proper grasping of power. "This is your priority. I want that boy back within a moon's cycle. The longer he is out there, the sooner another mage may find his power and seek to befriend him." There was a pause and Luthian returned to pacing, drink in hand. "I cannot believe you missed this boy's potential. It is bad enough you are incompetent with magic, to have missed this too is beyond redemption." Luthian was frustrated at his brother's ineptness. If not for the man's loyalty, he would have long since seen to an unpleasant accident. He could not believe that Henrick was born of the same loins for the two were not the least comparable. How could he have missed that his son was coming into power?

"You make it sound as if I have been negligent, Luthian. I have tested him every year. If you wanted more testing, maybe you should have just made sure that he was always on my route." Henrick looked from the fire to Luthian. His eyes were piercing and cold as he lifted his gaze to his brother.

Luthian took a step back for he was sure for a moment he saw contempt before it was hooded away. "You forget your place in the tiers, brother!" Luthian snarled working to exert his authority over his brother. Only once had Henrick challenged Luthian and in that battle, Henrick had been forced to his knees by his brother's powers. Luthian smiled with memory at making his brother kiss the toe of his boot in exchange for his very life. That had been the last time Henrick had ever shown any ambition, and that had been long before Luthian had become minister.

Henrick dropped his eyes in deference. "You are right. Maybe I am just upset at myself as well. In addition, as I said, I have not been well." Henrick carefully rose to his feet. "When do you wish me to depart?"

Henrick's voice was veiled, but Luthian could feel a boiling of emotion behind it. Luthian eyed him. "As soon as you see a healer and ensure you are ready for the trip."

Henrick bowed although not as low as usual. "It shall be as the minister commands." Henrick turned and swept from the room not waiting for his brother's response. Though his words held the proper content, the contemptuous way that Henrick twisted the word minister sent a shiver up Luthian's spine.

Luthian frowned, watching him go. It was time to consider getting rid of his brother. He had the distinct feeling he was becoming a threat.

Chapter Eight

Alador stood in the bathing house as his brother kept moving about and chuckling. He stared at the steaming water and thought about the last time he had been here. Since the day the pool had boiled, he had taken to bathing in the river. The water did not feel as cold to him as it used to, and he did not have to fear being scalded. He was completely befuddled at the moment. He had no idea why these things were happening. He should be happy, but he felt more out of place than he ever had. His whole life seemed to be turning upside down. His thoughts drifted as he stood in the steaming room. It felt comforting as the steam swirled about him.

Almost every day in the village had been a challenge from the time he was old enough to know he was different. He remembered the first time he had come to blows with Trelmar. He and Gregor had been playing by the river in a small eddy that was shallow. The elders hovered close by to make sure none ventured past the marking stone. Gregor had been chasing Alador, and he had strayed close to the marking stone. The river moved a bit faster here, and something shining had caught his eye. He had reached down to pick it up. There in his hand had laid a kingstone. Kingstones were clear like glass and shimmered in the sun. Trelmar had grabbed it out of his hand.

"You are not fit for a kingstone. My maman says you are soiled and not fit for the gods' blessings. Nothing but a foul Lerdenian!" Trelmar's tone had been full of venom.

Alador sighed softly remembering how he had stood confused looking down. He had been quite clean, and he remembered not understanding what Trelmar had meant. It had been the first time he had fought Trelmar. A fight had broken out in the water between Trelmar, Alador and then Gregor and one of Trelmar's friends. The elder that had pulled him out of the river scolded him for being aggressive. It was the first time he had realized he was different.

After that, he had learned how to cope and adapt to the criticism of his parentage. He knew what routes to take to stay out of Trelmar's path for the most part. He had learned to fight and defend himself to the point that Trelmar had quit attacking him alone and now would only seek Alador out if he had his group of followers to back him up. It had been one of the many reasons he had asked his father to take him with him when he came to visit.

He now was headed for everything he had ever wanted. He was going to be recognized as a true adult of the people. He would only have to work to the welfare of the village as a whole, or if he chose, he had enough slips never to have to work again. He should be happy. He would even have a real chance to be Mesiande's housemate. He smiled at the idea of sharing a home with her. Surely, even Trelmar would now have to leave him alone.

"Come on lad, strip down and get in."

The voice startled him from his thoughts, and he jumped in response. Dorien chuckled as he placed meraweed onto the hot stones almost immediately filling the room with the relaxing vapor. Dorien was already stripping down to slip into the steaming hot water. Alador gradually followed suit. He frowned for his body was slight in comparison to his brother. Daezun had a sturdy body to begin with, and the fact his brother was a blacksmith only added to his physique. His muscles stood out and were defined on his chest. Patches of the thick, black chest and arm hair were missing due to burns while blacksmithing. These patches were white against the otherwise tanned body of his brother. Even with the scars, Dorien drew the eyes of the village women when he pulled off his shirt. Alador slipped into the water after his brother, sighing with pleasure. Both brothers just lay back in silence for a long while.

Alador realized his brother was watching him just before Dorien spoke. "Alador, how did you repel that dragon?" His brother leaned back against a stone seat watching his younger brother with curiosity. His tone held no accusation.

Alador looked over at him and sighed. "You would not believe me." How could he tell his brother he was had heard a voice? Or had it been some innate knowledge? It had seemed like a voice. He had known to trust it. Was he losing his mind? It was known that some of Lerdenian mixed blood became rattled in the head when they came of age. Perhaps this was what it was like: Voices telling you what to do. Strange dreams that felt so real that you were not sure they had not just happened.

"Try me." Dorien encouraged. "We are alone. No one will come in knowing we prepare for your ritual. I have never heard of a dragon repelled with a single arrow. What did you do?"

Alador sighed. "I shot it in the mouth as it opened to draw air for its breath. The throat within has no scales to protect it." Alador was staring at the vent of warm water bubbling out of the bottom of the pool. His words were monotone as they spilled from his lips. His gaze was slightly absent.

Dorien was silent for a long while. His eyes were large and his mouth agape. "How did you know that? I do not recall much in our lessons on fighting such beasts for they leave the Daezun alone for the most part. It is usually only in the most dire of winters that they even raid the villages." Dorien handed his brother soap and a rag.

Alador took the rag and began to soap himself. "I must have heard it somewhere." He answered in a murmur. He could not tell his brother about the prompting. His brother would think he was losing his senses. By the gods, he thought he was losing his mind. It would seem worse to have it leave his lips, it sounded insane in his own head. His heart was racing, and he silently begged the gods to have his brother leave this line of questioning.

The two settled into silence. The mist swirled about with the vapor of the meraweed and sometimes it was so thick he could barely see his brother. The sound of the water gurgling up from the ground beneath and the fire under the hot stones were the only sounds as Alador finished bathing.

Finally, his brother spoke again. "Gregor tells me that since you smacked your head that you have emerged as a dead shot with your bow. Is this true?" Dorien's tone was no longer gently prodding. His brother's tone was curt.

Alador grew wary. His brother's tone and questions were as if he knew that there was something wrong with Alador. He looked over at Dorien before ducking under the water to rinse off the scented soap. He wiped his face clear of water before answering his brother. "I have been practicing hard. I want to be a guard when I enter the circle, so I have been at it every day." He let out a barely contained breath, unable to look his brother in the eyes.

Dorien sighed softly. "There is something I need to tell you Alador. If it is true, you must not tell me. When you were a small one, there was another of half-blood. He came into his magic around the time of your own age. I wondered when I saw the clear color of your stone if perhaps you have gained this ability. I have never seen a stone after its use, so was uncertain if something magical had happened. The day when the boys got burned, and you were not even reddened raised another concern..."

Alador could not look at his brother. It was clear he knew that something had changed the day he had pulled the stone from the ground. He shifted uncomfortably as his brother continued.

"To be honest, when the trader was willing to buy the stone, I was very relieved. Gregor's mentioning of your changes in the skill at shooting your bow a further point that I have added to the puzzle. Today...today was uncanny. I know of no one who has beat off a dragon with a single arrow. "Dorien looked at him. "If you have gained the skills in magic of your father, you will be cast off. If this has happened, you must hide it if you want to stay with kin and your Mesiande." Dorien's tone was cold in the last sentence. His words digging deeply into Alador's heart.

Alador winced and began to defend himself, but Dorien raised his hand to silence him. "I love you, little brother. You have ever been dear to my heart with those silver eyes of yours. However, if the village comes to discover any affinity to magic, I will turn my back on you with the others and deny I ever knew." Dorien's tone was a matter of fact. It brooked no argument. Alador could go to his father, Dorien would just become an outcast if he did not deny his brother. "Tell no one of this. Miss a shot here and there if this is from some insight of magic. If I am right and have pieced this together, I may not be the only one. No accusation will be made by any on mere suspicion. They will have to have proof. Step wary brother. It would break maman's heart if you were to become an outcast. For all her bluster about your parentage, she always becomes most happy when your father visits." There was a sense of urgency and a tinge of fear in Dorien's tone.

Alador was speechless. His brother had never said he had care for Alador. The words of love had never been spoken. Yes, he had watched over him as a small one. He had teased and played with him as any brother. His eyes widened as he slowly realized that while his brother had not ever said such things, over time he had shown it. Memories of laughter and of patience, when he broke another handle trying to learn to blacksmith swept through his thoughts. "I will not forget your words." He eventually answered. He could feel the meraweed's relaxing effect steal over him.

A tense silence was as palpable in the room as the steam was visible. It was clear that his brother was upset. Alador decided to change the subject. "Dorien, why do the Daezun hate magic so? Is it because they cannot use it?" Alador had never dared to ask the question. Elders taught small ones early not to ask questions of that which is not taught. When learning, one was expected to stay to the topic being taught, and discussion of alternative points of view were often dissuaded as well. It was just the way of the people.

Dorien considered his response very carefully. "Name the gods as best you can, Alador." Dorien looked to his brother. "I will answer your question when you have done so."

Alador takes a moment to focus, a difficult task given the meraweed filling the room. He puts up his fingers and begins to count them off. "Detharo, Lyiu, Oessyn, Niaet, Rian…" He stopped and counted his fingers with a frown. "Krona, Hamaseic, and…Reistare." He names off the last three and looks up pleased with himself. "Why do you ask?" It seemed such a strange question to answer his own. What did the gods have to do with the Daezun hating magic? He tried to focus on Dorien through the haze of steam and vapor.

"Each of the gods decided that they would send a representative of themselves into the world of Vesta to watch over the mortals in their keeping." Dorien began. His voice was any other history teller around the fires. While the histories of the people where written, most often they were still passed down in front of a warm fire.

This was a tale that Alador knew well. He interrupted his brother with apparent irritation. "I know this, this was the birth of the dragons. Every small one knows this tale. I do not see what that has to do with the distaste of magic?"

Dorien put a hand to still his brother's speech. "Patience brother, patience." Dorien laid his head back and closed his eyes. Only when he seemed truly settled did he go on with his tale. "There is more to the tale that one does not learn until you are an adult. The dragons chose those sworn to their protection, and gifted them with magics. Two groups began to emerge. Some were greedy and constantly sought favor for more power. Some would refuse this gift of power in reverence to the gods' representatives. You see, when a dragon gifts power to a mortal, it loses some of its own. One day, the leader of those that would become Lerdenia demanded magic of a young dragon. When the dragon refused, he grew angry and slayed the one he had been sworn to protect. As he stood in the dragon's blood, he slowly absorbed the power of this dragon and became the greatest known mage of the Lerdenian people."

Alador listened forcing his attention on his brother. A difficult task given the intoxicating air they were breathing. He had never heard this part of the tale. It always stopped with...*and this is why we respect the dragons today. They are descendants of the gods' representatives in this world.* It never had occurred to him that there was more. It had seemed complete. It had made sense. Why were they not taught this part of the lesson? "What happened?"

Dorien was obviously struggling with focus as well, and he sighed softly. "A war broke out. Those that served the dragons in truth fought to protect them, and those that served themselves fought to slay them for their power. Those that protected were outnumbered, and so most of the dragons took flight and scattered about the world leaving the Great Isle far behind. Daezun hate magics for they were stolen through betrayal and blood. We do not learn this as small ones for small ones should not learn to hate." Dorien's tone was bitter.

Alador was quiet for a moment. He remembered his own travels as a small one. They learned hate just fine without this story. Slowly his next question formed as Dorien still sat with head back and eyes closed. "Why do they need the stones today then? Why do Lerdenians not just kill the dragons for their power?"

"A good question. The gods learned what the Lerdenian's had done and so lay a curse upon the dragons that only the oldest of each of the clans could gift power to a mortal. All other dragons' magic would be returned to Vesta that magic never be lost to those of mortal kin. Lerdenian's would see every dragon dead that their magics could be harvested, but they miss one important point." Dorien pointed out, his tone held contempt as he paused.

Alador looked to his brother, slightly disconcerted by this tale. He had mixed feelings. His father was of a race that had betrayed the dragons. The Daezun held most of magical skill in disdain. He had always wanted to be like his father but now, did he want to walk with those that were traitors to a task given to them by the gods themselves? He swirled his finger in the water as he realized that Dorien was not speaking. He looked at him considering his questions when they had first entered the pool. Alador had been different since he had held that stone. Had he stolen magic from a dragon? "What was that?" He finally asked softly.

"When the last dragon falls, when the last bloodstone is harvested, magic will die. Dragons *are* the source of magic. Magic is harvested from their pain and death." Dorien spat out the essential point.

Alador panicked. He had sold them a great sized stone. It must have held great power. "Then why do we sell Lerdenia bloodstones? Why do the Daezun not protect the bloodstones and hide them from the mages?" Alador asked with alarm.

"We only mine stones of fallen dragons. We do not shoot them and let them decay into the ground to form the stones. That is the way of Lerdenia. By supplying Lerdenia with stones, there are less dragon hunters to harm those that still dwell in the world." Dorien pointed out. "In exchange, we stand ready to protect the dragons. It is why there was so much shock today." Dorien paused. His face held confusion and concern. "It would seem the dragons are slowly forgetting their oath and the people that have always revered them for what they are, representatives of the gods themselves. There will be many people today wondering if they have angered the gods, and whether this was retribution."

This connected many things for Alador. He understood the mining better. He understood the distaste of the people for Lerdenia. He had thought it a result of the war, but it seemed that the blood that lay between the two people was that of dragons. He heart wrenched as he thought of the many that had died today. If the Daezun had always protected the dragons, why had the red dragon betrayed that pact? Had he found it easier to shoot that dragon not because he was protecting the people but instead that the blood of his father longed to take what was not his to claim? A swelling of emotion clutched at his throat. Dragons were noble creatures. How could someone slay the dragons so selfishly? He said nothing as Dorien placed more Meraweed upon the fire. As the sweet scent swept over him, he laid back in the hot water lost in his thoughts.

He could see now why his brother had cautioned that if he came into his magic that he must keep it hidden. He was already seen as different. If he came into his power, then he would have to leave. Was his ability to shoot this power? Had this pool heating and the fact he had not burned, were they signs of this power? He must have dozed although he still felt awake as he was pulled into the world of the dragon once more.

Renamaum stood on the hill watching below. His father had ordered him to stay out of the conflict. The fate of magic lay in the hands of the mortals below. Some dragons did not listen. Some had fought by the side of those that honored the trusts of the dragons. It had been a risky and dangerous ploy. While the support of a fighting dragon was a great boon to those below, if a dragon fell than the enemy close by was quick to slice them open and bleed them onto as many mages as could move close. This strengthened those that fought. The battle was bloody. He could smell the blood on the wind. So sickening sweet was the blood of the mortal. It did not have the fresh flavor of the sea creatures that he preferred to hunt.

His father had called for the dragons to disperse. He had urged them to leave the isle they had always called home. There were many lands and many caves abroad. The fate of the dragons would be secured if they did not stay on the isle. His family was not leaving. His father had sworn he would continue to protect the mortals that fought for them as best he could. He had taught Renamaum the words of the creators. He had taught him the gifting of magic for one day the young blue dragon would guide the flight. Renamaum still did not see how they were protecting by refusing to fight. It was a lesson he had not yet learned. The dragon roared in frustration. There was only one thing he was certain of, you could not protect if you did nothing!

Alador started awake. His gasp of surprise bringing a look of concern from Dorien.

"You all right?"

Alador nodded. He was not willing to share the dreams with anyone. They seemed, important and he felt a need to keep them secret. He glanced at his brother who was still relaxing in the seat. Although, at the moment, he was watching Alador.

"Good, can't have you falling ill tonight." Dorien winked at him.

Dorien's words brought back the fact that they were in the hut to prepare for the ritual. He realized they had not yet discussed it. He suddenly felt a bit queasy. "What will happen in the ritual?" He asked, looking at his brother.

There was a very long pause as Dorien gathered his thoughts. "Even as we bathe, the women are readying the ritual hut. When we are done here, I will take you there. A chosen elder will join you and bring you to manhood." Dorien answered. "Then you will take the duties of an adult and can even start to build a home if you want for a future housemate. You have the slips so will not have to work as I am to ready such a home." There was a tinge of envy in Dorien's voice.

Alador missed it for in that moment he had been imagining Luciesa, a very aged elder. He groaned again at the idea of an elder joining him at all, let alone in the manner of glimpses he had stolen from the inner circle. "Why does it have to be an elder?" He wrinkled his nose in distaste.

Dorien laughed. "I remember feeling the same way." Dorien splashed his brother fondly, and his eyes danced with merriment. "I assure you, tomorrow you will not be complaining, brother." He splashed his brother playfully once more. "Right now you are the envy of every middlin. Enjoy it!" Dorien leaned over and added a bit more meraweed. "Obviously you need a bit more than most." He teased the younger man with a wide toothy smile.

Alador smiled for the meraweed did indeed lull away many concerns and, even with his worries and confusion, he could feel his body slowly relaxing. He tipped his head back enjoying the steam and the gentle movement of the water. His brother was silent, letting Alador relax. He closed his eyes and let the sleepy haze wash over him. Meraweed had the potential to sap one's very fears away. He decided to just let it work. With his eyes closed, the heavy vapor and the warm water swirling over his body, he slowly fell asleep.

"I tell you Pruatra, Keensight is power hungry and a fool." Renamaum snarled. He watched his mate closely as she stirred the water the three eggs were bathed in. Their steaming movements rocking the eggs gently. Her talon shimmered with magic as she heated the water about them.

He could not help but soften as he watched her. She was so careful and gentle with their eggs. He eyed them with loving regard. His fledglings would not become power for the mortals. He would not let them be sacrificed to the greed of Lerdenians.

As mortals drained the magics of the dragon race, it was slowly draining the magics of the world around him. He could feel the loss of each dragon soul. The carnage had slowed since the dragons had spread their wings beyond the Great Isle. When the last dragon drew its breath, the mortals would lose their own ability to touch the power of the great pool. All dragons knew how to reach this hidden place. They knew how renew the magics they were imbued with from birth. It could only be reached by flight.

It was the dragons that were able to drink from the pools of magic and spread its blessings about Vesta. Keensight focused on the betrayal of mortals to the ancient pact. Created by Krona, his was the way of death and destruction. His red scales a gleaming reminder of the embers that burned within him.

Renamaum remembered the people that had stood between his own father and the great mage who had stolen power from an alpha of the Black Flight. Renamaum wanted to bring back the time of alliance having an affinity for the desperate passions of the mortal races. In doing so, he would protect the future generations of dragons. He eyed the eggs. Each year there were fewer new dragons.

Pruatra looked at her mate. It had taken her some time to respond. Like her mate, she was blue in scale and power. Unlike him, her body was lithe and snake like. A trait from her father whose purple and black scales had appealed to her mother. Her voice, a sultry purr that mirrored the way her tail slightly flicked back and forth had ripped him from his thoughts of the past and what was to come. "Perhaps Keensight has the way of it. Maybe we need to rid ourselves of this mortal race and keep our children truly protected." Her tone became calculating and held an edge of judgment as she spoke.

Renamaum stared at her in disbelief. His deep throaty tones took on an edge of a growl. "Pruatra, surely not you as well? Without the mortal races, what is to keep us from reverting back to the beasts they believe us to be? They create items of great beauty. They sing songs of passion and sorrow. These are things I would have my fledglings see."

Pruatra looked over to the mound of gold and gems interwoven with sea grass that made their bed. She loved such things. Renamaum knew how much she loved her treasures. These things would be lost to them if the mortals fell. There would be no new sunken ships to raid for treasures lost to the mortals. He watched the battle within her, apparent by the difference in the flickering of her tail. No longer did it dance for him but rather flipped back in forth in agitation. He could tell a *lot by her tail. He smiled as she growled in frustration for it meant she would concede his point.*

"All right, go to the council and know you speak for me and our fledglings. But know this, if any mortal touches an egg of mine or the fledgling of our mating, I will kill a thousand fold for retribution of what was lost." Her growl filled the cavern to emphasize her point. Her tail moved about in the water to swirl protectively about the three eggs that rocked from the movement of the water.

Renamaum knew better than to push his mate. He also knew she meant every word she had just uttered. She did not hold the mortals in favor in any way. Not even those that refused to steal from the dragon race's blood. He turned his bulk and slipped into the water that hid the entrance of their cave. He had to convince the rest of the gathering that there was another way. A war on mortals did not need to be declared. He had to save not only his fledglings, but the magic of all mortal fledglings to come.

"Alador, come on lad, wake up! It is time." The feel of something lightly tapping his arm brought Alador jumping up and looking about in a bit of a panic. He searched for dragons in the steaming water.

"Easy lad, you fell asleep." Dorien put out two hands in a non-threatening gesture. His usual warm smile was on his face, and he clearly looked amused at Alador's reaction.

Alador was breathing heavy as he looked about. He gradually came to some sense, but the meraweed was heavy in the air and his reactions were slow. The room cast in the steaming of the bath was much like the water that had moved between the two dragons. His brother standing there looking slightly amused helped to bring him back to reality. He slowly nodded to Dorien to indicate he was aware of where he was.

His brother crawled out and wrapped a towel about his waist then held out a towel for Alador. "It is heating up again. I don't want to get burned so let's not take any chances. Besides, I believe we have been in here long enough." Dorien frowned down at the pool. "I will see if there is something that can be done to divert the heat if this is going to continue."

Alador swiftly crawled out and began to towel off. Dorien eyed his brother and then smiled slightly. "Maman brought the ceremonial clothing." Dorien nodded to a small pile on a nearby stool.

Alador looked horrified. They had not been here when he had fallen off so his mother must have brought him when he was sleeping. He suddenly was glad for the steamy haze. Even if it was his mother, he had been naked. Alador toweled off and reached for the pants. He looked at them in shock as he held them up. "Th…these can almost be seen through?" He stammered out in alarm. The white linen was thin and soft but definitely somewhat transparent.

Dorien laughed. "You are not going to the mine, brother. Come on, get dressed. The robe will cover up a bit more. I find it hard to believe you are so shy about this. It is not like you have not been seated on the circle. I know you have to have stolen a glance." Dorien's face was lit with the amusement his tone of voice carried. "You would think you were some shy village maiden." Dorien punched him in the arm. "While I bet you have stolen a kiss or two."

Alador winced for his brother's loving taps were rarely as light as Dorien believed. "I have not." He defended quickly. "Mesiande would have punched me."

Alador pulled on the lightweight pants as his brother still laughing, also began to dress. He picked up the robe. His brother was right, the robe was slightly heavier and was also white. White was an unusual color and only worn for special events. Few Daezun owned their own whites, and so the clothes were often shared. The bleaching process took time so as not to damage the fabric. Most clothes were dyed to darker shades or where the natural cream color of the original cloth.

The rich embroidery on the robes held symbols that Alador did not recognize. When he was done, Dorien walked to him and placed a simple gold coronet upon his brow. It held no stones or symbols. It shined in the dim light, the steam on its metal surfaces catching the flickering lighting.

Dorien settled it in, but it fell over one of his eyes. His head was smaller than most Daezun and so the headband just laid there. Dorien chuckled. "I hope this is the only thing on you a bit small."

Alador rolled his eyes as Dorien adjusted it, so it rested across the center of his forehead. Alador stood uncertain before his brother feeling a bit uncomfortable. He shifted at the feeling of someone else touching him. The clothing felt far too light, and the coronet on his head seemed out of place. No adult ever told a middlin about this night. He had never seen a man emerge from the bathing hut for their ritual. He put a hand to the coronet when Dorien let it go and looked up to his brother with apparent hesitation, and his face held his discomfort.

Dorien nodded with approval looking his brother over. He eyed his younger brother for a long moment then went over to a satchel that sat near the seat his ceremonial clothes had been laid out upon. "Here, drink this." He gently shoved a vial into Alador's hand when he returned.

"What is it?" Alador uncorked it and sniffed it carefully. It smelt much like the meraweed vapor that filled the room but there was something else. A sharp stringent smell that reminded him of the healer's hut was blended in it. He held it up to gaze at it. Its amber hues in the little glass vial for flecked with darker spots.

"It is the drink that men take the night of circle. It helps a man mate several times" Dorien grinned at him. "It will also help you not care that there is an elder in your bed." Dorien added as if it was a bit of an afterthought.

For that reason alone, Alador swiftly drank it down. He coughed at the bitter bite that it left in the back of his throat. He stood waiting for some magical effect but other than his stomach churning, he felt nothing. He set the vial on the chair. The idea of an elder touching him or even seeing him in these clothes still seemed quite horrid to him. Why couldn't it have been an adult? At this moment, it seemed a much better idea.

Dorien moved a rug on the floor and opened a trap door. The door creaked as the heavy wood was lifted from its secure foundation. "This way to the ritual hut Alador." Dorien nodded that he should go down inside.

Alador just stared at him. He had been in this hut so many times. He had never known there was a door there. Then again, it never occurred to him to move the rug. Only the adults were assigned to clean and maintain the bathing hut, now he knew why. He walked to the hole in the floor and looked down. It was a lit passageway that led off from the bathing hut.

"Come on now, let us not keep the council waiting." Dorien shooed him on down the stairs.

"The whole council comes to watch?" Alador's voice hit a higher octave as he stood rigid at the edge of the stairs.

Dorien laughed hard. He had to wipe his eyes he was laughing so hard. Finally, when he could not stand the look of fear on his brother's face anymore, did he offer a bit of a balm. "Not literally. I have to go and tell them you are ready and then they will send in the chosen elder."

Alador climed down and stepped into the cool tunnel. The floor was lined with well swept stones and the walls were marked with symbols much like those on the robes. His brother was still chuckling as they moved down the corridor that seemed to run beneath the village. He couldn't tell which way they were going. The passage way was lit by torches as he walked down it to another set of stairs. He climbed back up through a second open trapdoor. He stepped into a room with a warm fireplace and a huge bed. The bed was covered in furs and blankets. A table was laid with food and drink as he looked around. He was the only one here, and he looked back at the trap door in confusion. His brother's head was visable at the top of the stairs he had just climbed, Dorien's hand reaching for the corresponding trapdoor. "What now?" Alador asked. He looked about with fear as he realized that while he knew what was the end plan, he had no idea what would happen in the beginning. His brother was leaving him, and he had a sudden desire to flee back down the passageway they had just come.

"The elder will join you shortly. Get a drink, relax Alador. I promise you, this will not be a night you will regret or forget." Dorien winked at him and shut the trap, settling it back into the floor.

He felt strangely warm, and there was a stirring within him he didn't understand. Alador paced the room looking at the furnishings. He sat on the bed and bounced up and down on it a few times. It made him dizzy, so he stopped. After sitting stiffly for a bit and watching the door in the wall, he moved to the table of food and poured a chalice of honeyed mead. It was a rare treat, and he smiled as he sipped at it. It felt soothing to his stomach and throat after the bitterness of the vial that Dorien had given him to drink. He wasn't really hungry though everything looked incredible. When was she coming? Why were they taking so long? It seemed like it had been at least an hour since Dorien had left. He looked at the trap door and once again seriously considered fleeing back down it.

He walked back to the big bed and ran his fingers along the soft furs. His own bed was a mere narrow board with a thin mattress pad made of old blankets sewn inside a covering. This mattress was clearly stuffed with something far softer for his hands almost sank into it. He had never seen a bed like it. His mother's was fairly nice, but its mattress was softened prang hide and termin feathers. He sat on it once more. He sipped the mead and watched the door in the wall. He wished it was Mesiande that was going to step through it. He imagined unbraiding her long hair and running his fingers through it. He smiled at the idea of laying her down upon this soft bed and slowly kissing her.

The door opened and Alador jumped up, spilling some of the mead on his robe. He cursed softly for these were not his and looked up in embarrassment. Meradeth stepped in and closed it softly. Alador stared at her. He had always seen her as old, an elder. Even when she had guarded the children when the dragon had attacked, he had seen her as merely one of the elders. In that moment, she did not look old. Her hair was loose and brushed until it shined. Although there were streaks of grey throughout it, let down it seemed more to enhance her face. Her body was clothed in a simple white robe much like his. It dropped into a v between her breasts. Although she was older, unlike Luciesa, she was not wrinkled or unpleasing to look at.

Meradeth came towards him as he stood with the chalice of mead in his hand trembling, his eyes watching her every movement. She smiled at him, and when he went to speak, she put a finger to his lips. She took the chalice from his trembling hand and walked back to the table to set it down. She moved back to him with a graceful manner. Meradeth ran her hands slowly up his chest. "Do not worry, Alador. I will be gentle." She whispered and leaned up to grace his lips with her own. Something lurched inside of him, and his eyes widened at the feeling. She slowly stepped back and dropped the white robe off her shoulders then slowly it fell to the ground. He stood staring at her for he had never seen a woman naked so boldly. Every middlin snuck looks at the women when they could, but he had never had a woman stand before him so openly.

Her body was still firm from years of village work. Her breasts were the only sign she was not an adult. They drooped slightly but in that moment, she seemed the most beautiful thing Alador had ever seen. He stared at her in amazement as she walked to him. She pushed him back onto the bed so that he sat before her and Alador did not resist. She ran her hands up his thigh bringing an immediate response from his body. Her lips claimed his and much to his surprise, she touched him, bringing him to full readiness. Something inside him seemed to snap, and his eyes flew open. He growled against her lips, and his arms went about her hungrily with that feral sound. Meradeth cried out in surprise as he pivoted and rolled her onto the bed.

Renamaum spied the lithe blue dragon frolicking in the water. He had smelled her on the air and knew she was ready for mating. Her eye was drawn to his own as she took to the air. He chuckled and thrust up off the ground after her. He loved a little chase from a mate. She was fast and agile. Renamaum banked and turned trying to catch the female. He smiled as she climbed higher and higher into the sky. The two dancing about one another, him grabbing for her and her dancing out of his reach as they spiraled up.

When they could not go much higher, she taunted him, flicking her tail into his face playfully. Renamaum growled and grabbed the tail. The female roared in surprise as she beat her wings to escape him. He used the tail to pull her slowly to him, and when he had her close enough, he lunged, wrapping her into his grip and wings. As he took her, they began to fall spiraling to the earth, his wings holding her close to him. Their bodies hurled writhing through the air towards the ground beneath them. Caught so strongly in his embrace, she was captive to his passions and his grasp made clear who was master. It was not until their death seemed almost certain that the great dragon thrust her away and both their wings snapped open, and they soared back up into the air. Renamaum almost hit the ground having held her a bit too long, and his talons whipped tree tops. The female had safely banked back around to land beside the pool, panting heavily. Renamaum banked and landed roughly beside her, sand flying at the impact. The female looked at him haughtily and with feigned disdain, turned as if to take flight once more. "Oh, we are not done yet." He growled. He pounced upon her before she could take flight, pinning her beneath his great weight.

Renamaum used his teeth to grab hold of her neck to hold her firm as he used his talons to move her tail taking her there on the ground. Pinned down, he sank into her as she was held with her back to him, his muscular flanks moving with the power of an aged dragon. Although she teased us if she was not willing, the female dragon gave to him on equal ground. Finally, there was no need to hold her for the needs of mating began to overtake the needs of play.

Meradeth went to move from the sleeping man's side. Her body well used by his need. She eyed the table of food and drink, and then him once more. Carefully she began to slide from the bed so as not to wake him.

Alador's eyes opened still glazed by the vision that had seemed to blend within his own love making. Her back to him much as the female in the vision, as he had followed the dragon's need. He could no longer tell what passions were his and what was the dragons. All he knew was that he wanted her, needed her. "Oh, we are not done yet." He growled out as he pulled her back to him, rolling her beneath him.

Meradeth giggled as he rolled her back onto the bed. "I am the one supposed to be teaching you." She whispered up to him. The hunger on his face made her eyes widen.

Alador claimed her lips hungrily, he did not want to talk. He wanted more. He needed more. Now he understood what his brothers had meant. He did not care that it was an elder in his bed. He did not care how old her kiss or touch was. He faded back into the shared mating. The evening became a flurry of writhing bodies, talons and tails, hands and lips.

The two dragons mated with abandonment at the side of the lake. The sounds of their lovemaking echoed along the water's edge. Prang and korpen alike, wisely wandered in opposite directions. The frantic need of the pair left small trees torn up, and the edges of the lake were scarred with the movement of their bodies and claws.

Later as the two lay tangled on the sand by the lake, the female nuzzled him. Renamaum growled tenderly and nuzzled her back content to lay in the warm sand and rest with his new mate. "What is your name?" He hissed, almost as a whisper.

"Pruatra." She answered softly, her tail flicking much like a cat pleased to have been given milk.

Chapter Nine

Alador woke the next morning alone in the bed. He smiled in memory of the activities of the night. Even with the overwhelming visions of the dragon, he now knew what his brother had been smiling about in the bathhouse. He was a man now, an adult of the village. He could build a house. He could choose how he would contribute. He had been thinking about this for some time. Now that he could shoot with a bow with such accuracy   He wanted to be a hunter. His shot with the bow had become deadly, and he rarely missed. Usually that was due to some distraction such as Mesiande poking him.

He got up. The room was in a bit of shambles, and he smiled remembering how it had gotten that way. There were no blankets on the bed, and one of the chairs had been knocked over when they had been at the wall. Dorien had said that the elder would teach him, but she really had not had much opportunity. She had moved them to different positions a couple times but mostly she had walked with him in his hunger. He did not know how else to describe it. It had seemed an overwhelming hunger. He eyed the table of food and the delicacies it contained. Now that one need was sated, he found that he was ravenous. He moved to the table of food and began devouring everything close to him. He could not remember ever being this hungry.

His thoughts drifted back to Mesiande. He had always enjoyed being with her. Lately, all she had to do was be nearby, and he was aware of her. He noticed things that he wasn't sure had been there before. Little things like the way she would move her hair out of her eyes, or when she had her hands on her little hips to scold him. Like most Daezun women, she was stocky and more than capable of holding her own in the mines, but the way her body moved and the curves that showed in her mining pants made him long to run his hands along them. He imagined her in his bed as the elder had been, his hands running over her naked body. He smiled, and his body stirred at the mere image of his Mesiande laying beneath him. It would not be wild when he took her to his bed. It would be slow and wondrous.

He was so lost in this vision of Mesiande that when the knock came at the door, he jumped knocking over the glass of juice near his arm. He realized he was naked and at that moment, a bit more noticeably so in response to dreaming of Mesiande. He glanced about wildly for clothing and eventually settled for wrapping a blanket about him before opening the door. Dorien just grinned at him and held out a pile of clothes.

"Brought you some clothes as I doubt you want to come to council in those pants you had on last night." Dorien winked at him, his eyes glimmered with amusement at the embarrassment of his little brother.

Alador turned a bright red and took the pile with his free hand without a word. The other hand was holding the blanket closed at his side. He could not quite look his brother in the eye, but it was more that he had been caught fantasizing then what had happened throughout the night.

"You alright? I mean you look a little flushed. Maybe I should send the healer in to check things out, make sure nothing is amiss." Dorien's eyes sparkled with mirth at the wide eyed look on Alador's face.

Alador was horrified at the idea of the healer running her hands over his body at the moment. He shook his head adamantly still not quite able to find his voice.

"When you are dressed, join us at the alehouse." Dorien turned and walked off chuckling at the look on Alador's face.

Alador stood in the doorway staring at his brother's back. It was only when he noticed a couple of middlins staring at him that he slammed the door shut in sheer embarrassment. He swiftly attempted to dress, hopping about on one foot to get his breeches on. Despite being alone, he had a sudden urgency to get dressed. So much so he fell over trying to get the second foot in.

He was surprised to see that the clothing provided to him was new. The leather britches were a warm brown. They had been worked to the point that the leather was soft and held none of the stiffness of typical fresh leather. The shirt was a darker brown linen. The leather cords were well tended, the two sides usually roughened in the cut had been rubbed smooth with wax. He finished pulling on the clothes and realized he had no boots. He had left them in the bathhouse last night. He should have grabbed them. It would not sit well with his maman if he had his boots stolen again. He frowned not really wanting to go to the alehouse barefoot. However, it turned out as he stepped out on the steps that his brother had seen to that as well. A pair of well worked leather boots sat upon the steps. He sat down and put them on. They fit well, and he wondered at how clothing had been prepared that fit so well and yet he had no knowledge of their making. He now was dressed as an adult and it felt strange. Most middlins wore hand downs that fit poorly and had patched holes. He had been wearing his brothers' casts off all his life. He had never had anything of his own other than his boots. He stomped the boots out a bit. They were stiff and not as comfortable as the pair he had left last night. He knew they would need broken in, but he planned to save them for more formal events and use his old ones in the field.

He walked slowly towards the alehouse. It was a beautiful morning. The sun was shining, and the sounds of those rebuilding from the dragon's fire could be heard. The hammering and sawing was the most prevalent sound. It was quieter than usual, but then that was to be expected given the deaths during the fires. The morning freshness was sullied by the scent of smoldering wood and scorched earth.

He nodded to other adults that were about and greeted him with a knowing smile. Some of the women were whispering and eyeing him. More than one seemed to be sizing him up, and he didn't understand what the looks meant. He looked down at his clothing, but he seemed put together well enough. He didn't see any of the middlins about, but he realized he really didn't want to answer the thousand questions he would be required to refuse to answer. He remembered asking his brothers both what had happened, and they had both smiled and said he would know in time. Now he would be the one answering with such a knowing smile.

He supposed that everyone knew what had happened, after all they were all brought into adulthood the same way. His eyes narrowed as he thought Mesiande. He did not like the thought of any male touching her as he had been touched. A soft growl emanated from his throat as he felt anger rise in him. The audible growl surprised him, and he looked around to make sure no one noticed. No such luck, he took a deep centering breath as he realized people were looking at him strangely. A couple of the women nearby giggled as they went about hanging out the morning wash. His brother had been right. If he did not hide his emotions better, he would be sent away. When had they changed? He had always cared for Mesiande and hoped to be her housemate, but there had been little hope in that, so he had remained the good friend. This wave of possessiveness, when had that started? He forced his thoughts away from Mesiande and back to the path before him. He stood staring at his feet, struggling to contain the strong feelings he was currently experiencing. He had never struggled much with emotions except when Trelmar was around. Lately, he seemed to be nothing but a torrent of feelings. He did not like it.

He forced himself to think on other things and started back along the path. What could be so important that he was being summoned to the alehouse? It was where the adults often gathered to speak of the day. Many trading disputes had been settled over a cup of ale. Meetings for the whole village were held in the circle. So this wouldn't be all the adults and elders for the alehouse would not hold them all.

When Alador got to the alehouse, his brother was lounging against the wall outside. Despite his relaxed posture, his body was tense. Dorien was not in his usual blacksmithing clothes but rather wore a similar set of clothing though his shirt was a deep green. His eyes were not full of his usual mirth and manner, there was a strange seriousness to them. Dorien clasped him around the shoulders with a warm smile that did not match the rest of his body language. "I do not know what you did this time, but it must have been really good!"

It was the only warning Alador had before he was ushered inside. Things were moving so quickly since the dragon had attacked. He let himself be guided inside without much thought or response. His eyes widened as he saw the inside of the alehouse. There was not the usual bustle of patrons and buzz of conversation. It was, in fact, very still with only a low murmuring. In the center, a long row of tables had been pushed together and at it sat the elders' council. A few of the leading adults were gathered about, as well. Alador's eyes were very large as he looked at the solemn gathering. He had expected to go to the alehouse for a celebration of entering adulthood. This was not what he had pictured.

Dorien's face fell as well seeing their somber gaze. "Or not." He muttered under his breath, but Alador still heard him.

Alador swiftly assessed the table to see if anyone else had heard Dorien. They did not seem to have, and as they moved more fully into the room, all eyes turned to the two young men. "Please have a seat." Velkar, the elder in the center of the council, gestured to two seats that were fairly centered before the table. His tone was not threatening, but it was formal.

Alador had only heard that tone once before, and that had been when a middlin had been sent to another village for being too forward with the females. Both men walked slowly to the indicated chairs and sat down gazing about the table somewhat worriedly. Alador folded his hands into his lap, more to keep them still than anything. His heart was pounding in his chest as the two sat before the council. The few adults in the room stood around the edges. They were armed and this concerned Alador very much. He met Dorien's gaze and saw the acknowledgement that all was not well.

As Alador looked around the table trying not to squirm under the council's assessing gaze, his eyes met those of Meradeth who smiled at him then looked away. *Well*, he thought, *it can't be that bad if she is smiling*. He smiled back remembering some of the moments of last eve. He could not help but notice she did not look quite so old this morning as she had just two days earlier. He was so lost in his thoughts that he did not realize for a moment that Velkar was speaking to him.

"Alador, while you were in ritual, the council met. There was a great deal of discussion of events as of late in regards to matters surrounding you. Your find, the bathhouse, and the dragon; there is a concern that some magical taint has been transferred to you due to the size of your bloodstone." Velkar's aged voice was slowly paced. His eyes had a hawk like quality as he peered over his narrow nose at Alador. Whether it was to make his point or because he could not see did not matter, Alador squirmed as if the man could see straight to his most inner thoughts. The rest of the council nodded somberly as Alador looked around the table and even Meradeth lost her smile as the accusation was laid before him.

Alador felt his brother kick him under the table even as he looked at Alador passively. He barely contained the cry that rose in his throat and so he coughed instead. Alador knew in that moment that not just his place in the village but his family's was also at risk.

Dorien did not deserve any taint from any actions that
Alador was responsible for and he had considered
Dorien's words from their previous discussion on such
matters. He had been different since he had found the
stone. Had his father's power finally awakened in him
from having touched such a large stone? He felt
something stir deep within as if he had called something
up. It was uncomfortable and hot. He pushed the feeling
away as he worked to answer the elder calmly. Panic was
what he felt but when he finally spoke it was calm and
very unemotional. "If this is true, Elder Velkar, then my
father's trip is around the time of circle. He tests me every
year to see if I have gained any such abilities."

"Yes, Yes. This is what we thought." Velkar
gestured to the council about him. "We will want, this
year, for your father's testing to be before the council."
The Elder said with a decided tone of finality. He eyed
Alador with that piercing scrutiny.

"Y-yes elder." Alador responded as he dropped
his eyes in deference. He was boiling with mixed
emotions. There was relief that they were not going to
cast him out with the random events that he, himself,
could not explain. But there was also fear, Dorien had
made good points yesterday, and it was very likely he had
finally awakened the magic within his Lerdenian blood.

"Do you feel different Alador?" Luciesa asked
quietly. She was second upon the council, and Alador and
his friends had often joked privately that her age could be
determined by counting her wrinkles. Of course, no one
could count all of them without losing track or showing
disrespect. She currently sat to the right of Velkar and
clearly had a more tender manner then the elder who sat
at her side. She and Velkar had been housemates and
really were inseparable in most things. However, it didn't

mean she didn't speak her mind against Velkar if she did not agree.

He did not raise his eyes for fear that the emotional turmoil that twisted within him would be seen. "I have felt overwhelmed since finding the stone, Elder Luciesa." He responded honestly.

"How so?" She asked with a smooth consoling manner. Her face may have been covered with age, but her eyes were as sharp as any adult.

Many elders at the table seem to perk up at his answer, and he could hear them shifting as this statement drew their attention. He glanced up, but Velker was still staring at him with that piercing uncomfortable stare. "A-as one of mixed blood, I have often stood on the edges. P-people speak to me now. I feel an acceptance that is new and somewhat alarming. I am used to being unnoticed." Alador struggled to speak calmly though his heart was racing. "I find such attention overwhelming." In an attempt to mask his fear, his speech was far more formal in tone and manner.

"I assure you, that after Maredeth's report from last night, no woman will look at you as unwanted any time in the near future." Jespian fired out, he was an elder with a sharp mind and slightly sharper sense of humor. He winked with a wicked grin at Alador.

Alador turned a deep red as laughter went around the table. The females of the room grinned at him While he was grateful for the focus to be taken off his potential use of magic, having his ritual put on the table was not much better. Even his brother chuckled at that, and no one seemed upset or alarmed by his somewhat feral behavior the night before. The only one not laughing was Meradeth who had turned as red as Alador. He met her gaze and finally grinned, and she did as well.

"He does take after me in some respects."
Dorien retorted, and the laughter went round again.
Dorien slapped Alador on the back in admiration.
Dorien's booming voice took the focus off Alador for the moment.

Alador, though embarrassed, was relieved that the tension had eased at the table. He knew that he was on dangerous ground if his father's powers had manifested. He knew now why magic was so hated amongst the Daezun. While those of mixed blood were included on the edges of the Daezun society, they were not truly welcome and often remained without a housemate. He could not imagine a life so lonely, the only companionship given by the ill and injured. He had Gregor and Mesiande growing up as well as his family so while still slightly on the edges of the social status, he had not felt totally alienated. Even with these small blessings, he knew he had not fit in. If he had magic, where did he fit in? His musings were interrupted as Elder Velkar began to speak again.

"Until we know the extent of the damage done by the stone, we will act as if there is none. You will be placed upon the watch over the Elders and small ones during the day. It will be your duty until your father's test. At that time, assuming all is well, you may choose your own path. This is the decision of the council." Velkar looked at him with more seriousness now that the laughter had ceased. The other elders nodded in apparent agreement. "This will free a man for the rooftops to stand watch and will give us time to assess your situation further." They usually did not have such a watch, but with the attack of the dragon, it was no surprise that one was being implemented.

Alador was relieved, he did not mention he had wanted to do just that. It had felt right to protect the small ones against the dragon. It had been almost instinctual to do so, and he breathed a sigh of relief at his assignment. In truth, the council was being quite generous with the suspicion that his Lerdenian blood was asserting itself. "I will be happy to serve in this capacity." He answered with a respectful dipping of his head.

Dorien smiled and looked at his brother for a bit. Some of the Elders were downing their drinks as if to leave. "Will he still be allowed in the circle, Elders?" Dorien's question stilled the movement of those getting ready to depart.

Jespian laughed. "We would be lynched in our sleep if we denied him." Jespian winked as color resurged into Alador's face. "News of his, uh, stamina has spread amongst the women like wildfire."

Alador groaned as everyone laughed once more. Even the adults were laughing heartily, and the alehouse owner, Mistress Belithes winked at him. He didn't look at anyone else for fear of meeting another female gaze. Mugs slapped the table in appreciation of Jespian's quip.

Velkar pounded the table to gain attention once more. "Elders, we are not quite finished here." Velkar looked up and down the table till all stilled once more. It took a few minutes for a couple of elders seemed hard press to stop chuckling. When it was finally silent once more, he turned his gaze back to Alador. "Alador, please tell the council what you did to repel the dragon." Velkar eyed him. The movement and humor settled as all eyes returned back to the young man sitting before them.

Alador swallowed hard and looked up and focused on Luciesa. She seemed less threatening to him. "I waited for him to open his mouth and breathe fire and then shot down his throat." He said this as if it was quite common. Everyone was quiet as they watched Alador and he shifted uncomfortably. He was uncertain what he had said wrong for the silence had gained an almost palpable weight.

No one spoke for a long time. Finally, Luciesa responded with a bit of kindness, "You understand if you had been wrong that the dragon would have consumed you in fire?"

Alador nodded slowly "I could not let him breathe for the small ones were behind me in the brush." He said firmly. "It seemed the best thing in that moment."

Velkar tapped his chin thoughtfully, his mind considering. "It has been several years since a dragon has attacked a village unprovoked. I find it odd that one has done so now. The gods have always protected the Daezun from the ire of dragons. Perhaps the times are truly changing." At first a few smiled, but the look on Velkar's face showed no amusement. Everyone was quiet as the elder considered the events before him. "Unless…"

At that word, Velkar's gaze moved to Alador and rested upon him. Alador swallowed hard at the deep scrutiny he was given, and his eyes dropped unable to hold either elder's gaze any longer. He did not know the elder's thoughts, but it felt as if they did not bode well for Alador. Luciesa reached up and placed a hand over Velkar's, drawing attention from Alador to herself.

"Surely more time must pass?" Luciesa asked Velkar. She looked at Velkar, a question in her eyes. Her soft question drew Velkar's attention from Alador.

Luciesa and Velkar exchanged a serious look, and a heavy silence hung over the table. All the elders were watching Velkar and Luciesa. Alador snuck a look in the continued silence. She shook her head slightly, and Velkar frowned. When finally Velkar spoke, it was as if the subject had somehow been resolved between the two. "We will spread the word of how you repelled the dragon. It is a dangerous tactic, but the information should be given to the other archers. I believe our questions for now are answered. We will await your father before any additional matters are discussed." Velkar nodded curtly. The other elders seemed to breathe a sigh of relief in unison.

"Yes Elder." Alador looked with relief to his brother. He could see the same relief in his brother's eyes. He slumped down in his chair slightly, feeling as if a large weight had been taken off his chest.

The elders began to murmur amongst themselves, and a couple of the adults moved to open the door back up to the village. Velkar and Luciesa were whispering, and both appeared to have a look of concern. Meradeth smiled at Alador and then rose and moved to leave the building.

Dorien nodded and clapped his brother on the back. "Well then Alador, my dear lad, I do believe you owe some ale to some miners, and I am sure the elders wouldn't mind a drink of your slips." He flashed Alador a look that Alador understood immediately. They both knew his position was very insecure, and some celebration and sharing of his largess could not help but soothe the tense waters they had just sailed through. "It is a fine day and one to celebrate." Dorien's usual loud and boisterous voice drew the eyes of all those in the large room.

Alador looked around the room and slowly smiled. It was true, despite the tension of the last hour, he was an adult now. "Ah yes, I did promise to share." He got up and walked to the bar, many of the elders watching him closely. He looked over at Mistress Belithes who stood drying a tankard. "Run a tab and I will pay you first thing in the morn, Mistress?" His tone was one of question and hope. He did not want to leave everyone and have to run home for slips.

Mistress Belithes tossed the towel upon the bar and began pulling up additional tankards. "Aye, for I know where you live and what drink your brother best keeps. I am sure if I cannot find you, he soon would." She grinned at him and began filling mugs. Alador and Dorien ferried them to the elders that hadn't hurried to the bar to be the first to share in Alador's good fortunes.

Alador had been rather surprised. He had turned with two mugs only to have them taken from his hand by grinning elders who congratulated him before drinking deeply and moving off. He had been surprised elders could move that fast.

Once that was done, Dorien went to the door and flung it wide. "The alehouse is open, and Alador is buying." There was a cheer that could be heard from outside. Having been waiting for the alehouse to reopen, it was not long before the room was filled with adults and middlins.

Alador eyes widened as he saw the number of mugs shared and passed around, many being refilled again and again. Unaware his brother was watching him, he jumped when his brother approached him and whispered in his ear. "Better a few slips and to be well thought of then too much merit in that testing."

Alador nodded. He feared they were going to drink the alehouse dry at this rate. Unable to watch more, he grabbed a mug for himself and went outside the bustling house. He looked around for Mesiande. He was surprised she had not been here. He sat on the stoop and sipped his own tankard. He now dreaded his father coming for his naming day. Always before, he had hoped to leave with his father one day. Now, now he wanted nothing more than to stay right here. He finally had a home, and it was now threatened by the very thing he had sought all of his life, a little magic.

Chapter Ten

Renamaum was meeting Pruatra by the small lake where they had first mated. He smiled as he hefted the large fish for their dinner into the air. She was heavy with egg and would soon lay. He planned to take her to the cave he had prepared. Its entrance was well protected. The cave did not even show to others except at the lowest of tides. At all other times, the entrance was under the water line. It then rose up from the sea and inside there was a small stream of fresh water. He had made a bed of the softest sea grass and sprinkled it with treasures from a nearby wreck.

This would be his first clutch, and whether there was one egg or many, he was looking forward to having dragonlings to teach. He would teach them the old ways and the pact made with the mortals that walked the isle. He would teach them the value of home and the bounties of the sea. So much world was out there to explore. And when it was time, he would take them to the magic pools to drink for the first time.

He roared with excitement and danced through the air. His wings banking left and right as he sought the updrafts, playing in the wind. He spotted the landmarks and began a slow spiral down. He knew she would love the fish, it was one of Pruatra's favorites. In addition, it was still cold and only recently had stopped twitching, the catch was fresh. Heavy with egg, she had not been as swift. He spotted her along the shore and then he noticed she was not alone. A large black dragon was faced off with her. He recognized the irritated twitch of her snake like tail, its blue scales catching the light as it moved back and forth.

He banked down hard and came in beside her with no grace. He dropped the fish a few feet before he hit the ground, so as not to damage it. The furious beat of his wings to slow his descent doing little to minimize the ground shaking impact. He eyed the black as he looked at his mate. "Problems, Pruatra?"

Pruatra blinked the eye near him in a lazy manner as she drew her head up. "It would seem this black seeks to take your place as my mate. Why even now he was regaling me with tales of your demise and the fine lair he has ready for my eggs." She looked at Renamaum with almost imperious consideration.

"My demise?" Renamaum rumbled with humor. "I see and may I ask how I have come to such a sudden end?" He moved a step forward as the black before him appeared unconcerned and presented as having little fear.

"Why I killed you, of course." The black dipped his head in acknowledgement ever so slightly. "It was a fine battle."

"Should you not actually fight the battle before you claim the prize?" Renamaum almost liked this interloper.

The black inspected a talon and then looked up at Renamaum. "I always find it easier than actually exerting myself if the prize can be convinced the battle is done."

Pruatra snorted with indignation. "As if I believed you. I would know if Renamaum fell, we are true mates."

The black peered at Renamaum. The blue dragon had drawn himself up to full form. Renamaum surveyed the black. His weapon was more deadly, the dripping acid could render scales nearly useless. It would make up for the fact that that the black was also somewhat smaller. He also knew the black flight could bank on a tighter round then he could. However, he and Pruatra outnumbered him, and that was a point he was hoping would put the dragon off. He didn't want Pruatra in a fight, but he also knew she was a willful mate and was likely to make her own choices in the matter.

"Pruatra, take a swim." Renamaum hoped she would get his message. The black dragon's acid was *diffused in water, but their weapon could be launched from within it.*

Pruatra gave an indignant sound of air as she turned and lumbered her body off the beach and into the lake. She submerged out of sight, and Renamaum knew she was safest there. Whether she would stay there or not, well that would be another matter.

Alador shook his head free of the strange vision that had caught his thoughts. He realized that he had not seen Mesiande. In some ways, the female dragon reminded him of her. He sat upon the steps of the alehouse gazing about the village as it moved and breathed with a seeming life of its own. He did not see her hovering anywhere. It was later in the day than he had thought when he first left the ritual hut. The sun was well past the high mark. The sounds of the repairs being made from yesterday's fire filled his ears. The village would send the dead to the gods tomorrow. Preparations were being made for funeral pyres. He had seen a korpen pulled by with a cart of boughs. It usually was two to three days before a funeral. There was a pyre to build and then of course the preparing of the bodies. With so much going on, maybe she had headed out of the village.

He stopped by the house for his bow and quiver, then he headed for the fields. It was a day of work, so perhaps she had not decided to help drink up his slips and had instead stayed to her duties. Most that had taken advantage of the free ale would also have only a cup or two and return to their tasks. He smiled at the thought of Mesiande sitting at his table, glass in hand. He kind of liked the idea of providing for her. He walked along happily, now on the task of seeking out the girl that held his thoughts. He knew she wasn't with Gregor because Gregor had put down two mugs of ale before he had wandered out.

Gregor had never been one to turn down free food or drink. He was usually first in line at any gathering where food was involved. He didn't seem to carry any fat and yet he could out eat Alador two to one on any day. Alador had long since learned not to try to outdrink him. He smiled remembering the time the two had snuck off with a small keg and worked to out drink the other. He had woken up in a dress. He still had no idea whose dress that had been.

He hopped the stone border that stood between the fields. Each field's border was built from the rocks that were cleared. It left the ground free for planting and given that Korpen were not prone to a great deal of effort, it kept wild herds out of the fields. Prang could jump, so they didn't even bother to keep them out. In fact, it made for easy hunting at times.

The crops were just breaking ground, and small green sprouts were within every row. The task at hand now was to thin where too many seeds had fallen to insure that the yield was strong and that the plants did not choke each other out. It was not work he enjoyed and would often volunteer to work in the forge. He would rather sweat in the heat of sun and forge then try to thin those delicate plants.

He nodded to several that were involved in this task, but he did not see her anywhere. He wandered the field to the far end towards the river. It was beautiful in the spring season. The trees were all full of bright green leaves, and the prickleberry bushes that grew along the outer border in places were awash with bright purple blossoms. As he made it down to towards the river, he saw two figures against a tree. It looked to be lovers. He started to turn another direction, and then looked back. There had been something about the girl against the tree that seemed familiar. His vision focused as it did on the targets, racing towards him. It was Trelmar and Mesiande. She had her back to the tree, looking very angry. Trelmar had one hand on the tree beside her head, her braid in his hand, and the other hand was stroking a finger slowly down her cheek. Mesiande was pressed back to the tree, her hands were tightly clenched. Trelmar's back was to him. His finger stopped at her lips, and Alador could see her trembling as if he stood beside them.

Rage flooded through Alador, and he began to run towards them. His eyes flitted between the ground he was crossing and Mesiande's face. He vaulted the stone fence that marked the field, and threw down his bow and quiver as he drew close. Normally, his bow was far too precious for such rough handling, but in that moment, Alador did just not care. He knew what Trelmar was planning. There was only one reason he would pin Mesiande against the tree like that. He tackled Trelmar just as the middlin was leaning in to take a kiss. Trelmar looked up just before Alador landed in the middle of him and tried to turn to fend him off. Mesiande's gasp of shock was lost as the two went rolling down the small incline tangled up in one another. When they hit the bottom, they both pushed back trying to untangle from the other. Both Trelmar and Alador rolled up almost simultaneously and squared off.

Trelmar grinned maliciously. "Finally a reason to beat you senseless as Mesi here is a witness that you started it." His tone dripping venom.

Alador didn't wait for further conversation. He had one desire, and that was to beat Trelmar senseless. The middlin had tormented him all his life, and now had dared to touch his Mesiande. He launched himself at Trelmar, trying to smash him in the face with his fist. Alador's intent was clearly broadcasted, and Trelmar was quicker than him and so easily blocked and sidestepped. Alador felt the blow to his ribs as his breath left him. Trelmar spun about and kicked him further down the incline toward the water. Alador barely kept his feet attempting to catch his breath, his lungs felt on fire.

"Stop it! Stop it both of you!" Mesiande picked up a rock and threw it hard, catching Trelmar in the shoulder. "I will fetch the elders, I swear I will!!" Mesiande screeched at them both. Her eyes wild with panic.

Neither man seemed inclined to pay much heed to her as the bully strode towards Alador. Trelmar didn't even glance at Mesiande when the rock hit him. Trelmar had beat him so many times before, but this time Alador felt no fear. He heard the man coming as he was trying to draw air and Alador managed to turn and as Trelmar launched himself at Alador's back. He grabbed the man's arm and using his forward momentum, managed to swing him into the river. Trelmar was caught unprepared and landed face down into the water, the splash sending water over Alador, as well. The river was waist deep and fairly swift.

Trelmar came up sputtering as he sought to gain footing against the current, his eyes filled with hatred. "You will never have her. You know this, right? Once I tell what you have done, they will send you to live in another village. I will take her as my housemate. No one will want her once they know some Lerdenian half breed

149

soiled any small one's she might have." Trelmar's sneering tone was cutting, and even Mesiande put her hands over her mouth. Trelmar pushed the hair out of his eyes so he could see. "I will make sure every night she curses the day she met you." Trelmar's eyes raked over Mesiande, his meaning clear in his undressing gaze.

That threat was the last thing Alador remembered. He launched himself at Trelmar where he stood in the water, and they both went under. The river current grabbed them as they fought. Each struggled for footing to have the leverage enough to hit the other. Blood filled the water near them as they became a tumbling mass of fists and fury. The frothing and splashing mass was being taken downriver. Mesiande ran down the bank shouting as they fought. Neither heard Mesiande underwater, and they were gasping for breath each time they came up. The river pushed them over rocks as the two were banged and carried through the small rapids towards the small lake downstream. As the two fought, another battle filled Alador's head melding with his own flying fists.

"You could just fly off and let me have her." The black drew back slightly, his hindquarters tensed to spring into the air. "It would save us both a lot of time and energy."

"I am afraid she carries my clutch and I am rather partial to the idea of raising them." Renamaum moved ever so subtly, ready to pounce. He would not make the first move of aggression. It was not his way. However, he was not afraid to defend what was his. She

was his mate, and no slimy black was going to worm in and take her from him, especially when Pruatra didn't want him in the first place.

The black used this moment to strike. He thrust forward and up just enough to attempt to rake his talons across Renamaum's eyes. The massive black wings, down thrusting with power enough to bend the small saplings nearby.

Renamaum had been ready and rather than ducking down, he twisted and grabbed the leg above the talon. He did not want the black in the air if he could help it. He bit down hard bringing a cry of pain from the dragon above him. Wings beat madly as the black tried to free itself from the painful grasp of the blue dragon that held him.

Renamaum waited, knowing the black dragon would try to free himself with his breath weapon. The massive black wings above him beat frantically and finally he felt the black take the great inhale. Just as that inhale slowed, he let go of the black dragon's leg. The black dragon's acid spewed from its mouth but given that it had been beating its wing so frantically to get away, it shot forward and up. Renamaum immediately launched up into the air, as well. It would take some time for the acid to resettle and in that time he had a window to gain a further advantage.

The two dragon's spiraled up as they looked for an opening. Renamaum purposefully widened his bank slightly so that the dragon would perceive a way to get behind him. He counted on the black waiting for his breath weapon and giving chase. He under calculated the intelligence of his foe as the black suddenly came up from his left. The black had banked even tighter, and his talon raked across the fragile membrane of the wing.

Renamaum's scream of pain brought Pruatra's head out of the water below them. He could only hope she would have more fear for their clutch than his own well-being. Distracted by his mate, he almost missed another strike at his wing and was only able to bank his wing down at the last second. The black's vicious claws raked across his back scales, the sound echoing down below them.

Renamaum's growled out in rage. He was not going to lose his clutch to some acid dripping, arrogant youngling! He banked hard to the right, going the opposite way of their spiraling, and waited for the black to give chase. He floundered his wing slightly in hopes of seeming more damaged than he was. When the black was almost upon him, he took a deep breath and the anger within him boiled. When the black was confident he would hit him again, he folded his wings and let himself drop. It was only for a second, but it took him out of the black's grasp as he sailed in tight. As soon as he could see the talons, his wings snapped back open, and he gave a mighty thrust and steam boiled out. The black dragon had looked down to see where his prey had went and took the steam to underbelly and face.

Renamaum did not wait, his massive wings beat the air as he gained ground on the foundering and screaming black dragon. He grabbed the tail, biting down once more. The sharp razor teeth finding purchase between scales.   Once again, he folded his wings. He let his weight drag down the black dragon. Screaming in fear as they fell, Renamaum calculated the fall carefully. It was going to have to be close for this to work. The trees below him were coming up fast. When he dared not wait any longer, he let go of the black dragon and snapped his wings out. Despite his efforts to prevent his fall, he hit the trees and went sliding across the ground. The black hit harder. Uprooted trees lay around them both.

Renamaum managed to find his legs and get up to look around. He spotted his foe. One of the black's wings was bent oddly and he still lay panting. One did not leave a dragon foe behind. They always came back, and there was no honor in mercy. The black dragon found his own legs as Ranamuam lumbered to him. Renamaum's anger was great. This whelp had tried to take his mate.

The two dragons faced off as they circled one another. Plants and saplings were crushed under the moving bulk. Though the black was lighter in the air, Ranamuam had more grace upon the ground. Seeing an *opening he rushed in. The black rose up on its hind legs and met the large blue dragon. Both fought for purchase with their hind legs, and front talons raked and jaws fought to grab hold. Their tails cleared the vegetation behind them as the two large males fought for dominance. A battle that would only end when one or the other lay dead.*

Renamaum backed off, dropping to the ground. The two pivoted around each other the strong hisses and growls sending any animal nearby fleeing off into the distance. Renamaum feinted, and the black dragon rose up to meet him. It was then that Renamaum pounced, his horned head hitting the black just beneath the jaw. Only his tail kept the black dragon from falling back, but it was the opening Renamaum needed. He grabbed the throat of the black in his mouth and clamped down. The rich taste of magic and blood flowed over his tongue as he fought to get a better hold.

Struggling for its life, the black dragon attempted to claw at the eyes of his foe but Renamaum had already started shaking his head back and forth. Each side to side movement of the massive male's head tore deeper, until at last a gush of blood filled Renamaum's mouth. Renamaum did not let go of his tight hold, wanting to insure the male could not breathe one final blast of his acid weapon. There was only one end here, and it was death.

When the black finally went limp, Renamaum let him go and roared in victory. In the far off hills, many cries answered as dragons honored his cry. Renamaum turned to find Prautra. She lumbered her egg heavy body back onto the beach and was looking quite dejected. Renamaum moved to her, testing his wing as he did. He would have to be careful with it till he could fly to the pools of magic. It was damaged but not unusable.

The next thing Alador remembered was that he had Trelmar's boot knife at the middlin's throat. They were standing in knee high water just past where the stream tumbled into the small lake. Mesiande had a hold of the knife hand, and she was screaming at him to stop. Her words tore through anger and the dragon vision.

"You will be killed...stop, please! I do not want to lose you!" Her voice was filled with panic and fear. Her tear filled begging broke through, and he finally looked at her. Her face was stained with dirt and tears. Her hair was filled with twigs and leaves from tearing down the river bank after them, and there was blood from a scratch on her cheek. Her braid was coming loose, and some hair had fallen about her face.

Alador snarled and stood up, stepping back, the knife not breaking the skin of the man at his feet. The taste of his own blood on his lips as his nose was bleeding profusely. He wanted to rip Trelmar's throat out; feel the blood gush warm and pulsing from his body. There was no honor in mercy and the middlin had touched his mate. Trelmar fell forward and rolled away to lay in the shallow water staring up at Alador with a fear filled gaze. Alador gazed down at him with contempt.

"He deserves to die for touching you and all the misery he has caused me all these years." He wanted to. By the gods, the feeling of holding Trelmar's life in his hands was still calling to him. The taste of blood fueled both rage and the anger of the dragon in the vision. He snarled down at the man in the water, sounding more animal than Daezun.

Trelmar's panicked gaze flew to Mesiande as Alador stepped forward with the knife once more.

"She is right. If you kill me, you will die. They will hang you. You know the law. You can't kill me, can he Mesiande?" Trelmar looked to the girl for support although only a short time ago he had been the one preying on her. He was working to get his feet under him.

Alador kicked Trelmar as hard as he could. He caught Trelmar in the shoulder sending him crashing back into the water. Mesiande was sobbing beside him. He knew he could kill Trelmar without remorse, but he could not do it in front of her. The sound of her crying was ripping his heart even as he stood there trembling, knife in hand. She would blame herself, and he knew it. He tossed Trelmar's knife into the river.

"Stay away from me! Stay...away...from...her." Alador drew that out to emphasize his words. "You..." Alador reached down and grabbed his shirt pulling Trelmar part way out of the water so that only he could hear his harsh whispered words. "...ever touch her again, I will not hold back!" The two men's gaze met, and hatred danced between them. Alador knew by the look in Trelmar's eyes this was not over for either of them. He tossed him back down into the water.

He could hear Mesiande still sobbing. Alador turned his back on Trelmar and took Mesiande by the hand. "Come on!" Alador snarled. He literally pulled her out of the lake and then headed back up the side of the river leaving Trelmar glaring at their departing backs as he struggled to his hands and knees. Alador's other hand held his nose to stop the bleeding as he forced his way back up along the river.

Mesiande's crying gradually eased as they worked their way back up the hill that had led down to the lake. It was harder going up because the path here was more of a Prang trail and both were forced to concentrate on the climb. A difficult task for Alador as most of the way up the hill, he was still holding his nose. By the time they reached the top, Alador had quit bleeding and Mesiande had stopped crying.

They stopped at the top, both breathing heavily. Alador's ribs hurt, and the effort of climbing had made every breath feel as if a knife was inside, dragging across his lungs. He could not look at her for fear of breaking down. He was a turmoil of emotions. He had made her cry. He had wanted to kill Trelmar. By the gods, he still wanted to kill Trelmar. He was fearful of what would come next. He was fairly sure that Trelmar would keep quiet for fear of having to admit Alador had whipped him soundly. Alador winced as he returned to the fact that he had made Mesiande cry.

"Why did you do that, Alador?" Mesiande asked after she had caught a few breaths. "Why did you attack him like that?" Her tone held a bit of accusation and confusion as she looked at him.

"He was touching you and I could tell you didn't want his touch." Alador felt that rise of protective anger and tensed up, clenching his fists. He loosened his grip when she gasped for he was still holding her hand. He did not turn to look at her. He was still not in control of his anger and knew he had to look a mess. He started pulling her up along the river once more. "No one touches you." He spat out.

"I can take care of myself, Alador! I would have done something if he had actually tried to kiss me." She frowned at him slightly as he was still half dragging her up the path along the river. "You know I would have." Her tone was one of indignation.

"That is the point, Mesi, you should not have been placed in such a position. He was beyond his rights and just another demonstration of the bully that he has become. He goes unchecked, and no one has the courage to go to the Elders!   He should be put down like the rabid beast he is." Alador answered with a soft almost growling tone. Leave it to Mesiande to get mad because he had been protecting her. He just shook his head as he forged their path back up the river. He was surprised at how far down the river they had come. It had seemed to him as if only moments had passed.

"And you are an adult now that touched a middlin, which is punishable in its own rights." She fired right back. She was quiet as they forced their way around a prickleberry bush. When she spoke again, her tone was soft and had a touch of fear. "Alador, only the council has the power of correction." She frowned at his back as he continued pulling her back up the riverbank. He did not answer her, so she jerked her hand free and stopped. "Talk to me!" She demanded.

Alador stopped. He did not turn for a long moment gathering his racing thoughts. He sighed in defeat. He didn't want to fight with her. Slowly he turned to look at her. She looked so beautiful. Her face was flushed and her eyes swollen from crying. Her braids were ragged from snarls caught by thorns and had a few stray twigs caught in them. Other then when she had been dancing, he couldn't remember a time she had looked more attractive. "What do you want me to say, Mesi?" He asked softly. His heart lurched as he stared at her.

"Oh gods, you are bleeding." She hurriedly pulled at the hem of her tunic. It would not come free and in her desperation she pulled hard and ripped a bit too much. A bit of flesh showing down at her side near her waistband as she finished ripping a bit free. The river bank was sloped down to the water here, and there a small pool of water swirled before crashing over the next rock. They stood in a bit of a clearing that was protected from view by a copse of trees and pricklebushes.

He watched her as she bent down at the water's edge. She came back and gently pulled him down to sit on a fallen log so she could bathe the blood from his face. It had not been the first time she had doctored him up after Trelmar had set upon him. He did not protest. In fact, he was staring at her as if he had seen her for the first time. He noticed everything about her. The swell of her breast as she nursed over his face. The smell of sweat and field mixed with her musk was intoxicating. He swallowed hard at the rise of his body in response to the feel of her hand. He closed his eyes and breathed deeply, letting her work.

Only when a great deal had been wiped away, did she speak again. "I do not understand. Where did you learn to fight like that?" Her voice held a bit of her amazement. "You have always avoided fights with Trelmar in the past. Why would you...how did you?" She bit her lip and stared at him with large eyes. "Why would you risk your life?!" She yelled at him more like a scolding mother than the woman whose honor he had just defended. Her eyes were large as she stared at him. Their eyes locked and for a good deal of time, neither spoke.

Alador broke the silence as he reached out and tenderly touched her face as she stood before him. His hand then strayed up to pick a twig from her hair. "I want to be the one to kiss you, Mesi." He finally answered as he tossed the twig aside.

She blinked as she stared at him. She opened her mouth to speak, but he put a finger to her lips. "For once Mesiande, shut up and let me have my say." Her mouth snapped shut as her eyes searched his. "I want to be the one that holds your hand. I want to be the one whose shoulder you cry upon. I want to be...your housemate." He finally looked away unwilling to see the shock or refusal in her eyes. He took a deep breath. He had wanted for so long to say those words.

There was a heavy silence. It seemed to last forever, and a pain grew in his heart as he realized that she was going to refuse him. His heart began to race as panic set in. He should not have said anything. He should have just said he was protecting her from Trelmar. He was such a korpen's ass! Why had he not kept his mouth shut? His hands clenched at his sides in preparation for the blow that was to come. The nightmare was finally at hand, and despite all the times he had dreamed she had cast him aside, it had not prepared him for the turmoil gathering within him. He closed his eyes waiting for the words of rebuff or derision.

"I...I want that too, Alador." She finally whispered to him, reaching out to touch his face. Her touch was gentle as she caressed his cheek slowly.

Prepared for her refusal, words tumbled out his lips. "I knew I should not have said...wait what?" Alador's eyes flew to hers. Mesiande's eyes were wide and filled with a strange look of longing. He stared at her in disbelief. In all the times he had thought about this moment, in all the ways he had rehearsed it, he had never really thought she would accept him. "I...are you sure?"

Mesiande laughed softly as she rolled her eyes. "Well, that is a fine way to respond to a girl's accepting of your proposal."

"I didn't propose." He thought about his words. He chuckled nervously as he realized that he sort of just did. "Okay, well maybe I did but it was not how I meant to do so. My plan had been some picnic and wine." He frowned. "Well damn, I did propose." He was rambling. "I am sorry th..."

It was Mesiande's turn to stop his cascade of speech as she put a finger to his lips. Only when he was quiet did she lean up. Her movements were slow, and her eyes were locked with his. She gently replaced her finger with her lips. It was a soft fluttering of a kiss. He sat motionless, afraid to move for fear of breaking this moment; for fear of waking up. Her lips were warm and sweet. When she pulled away and stared into his eyes he slowly smiled, and she answered with her own mischievous grin.

"It can't be official yet. It has to stay between us for now. You cannot accept a housemate till you have been to the circle." He reminded her frowning. He realized in that moment he did not want her to go to the circle. He did not want another in her robes.

"I know." She answered. "It shall be our secret, and one I will treasure till the day I can announce my choice legitimately. Will we live with my mother and her housemate?" She looked at him. It was common for new couples to move into the home of the woman. It gave the house another male to help until the couple could save up enough to build their own home.

He grinned happily, he was glad now more then ever to have found that bloodstone. "No!" He watched as she looked disappointed. He knew that she was very close to her mother. His grin got even bigger. "I shall build you a house. I will start on it before the next season's circle." He pushed the hair from her face as he stared into her beautiful brown eyes. He took the strip of wet cloth and gently bathed the blood from the scratch on her face. "Tell me what you want your home to have and I will insure it will be as you wish." He promised softly.

Mesiande lifted a brow as if considering. "I do not know, sir. I mean, I have quite fanciful tastes." She walked away from him tapping her chin thoughtfully. Her back slightly to him, she looked over her shoulder to ask. "Are you sure you can afford such an offer?" Her voice was haughty like a couple of the village girls whose mothers had done well. But her eyes gave way her teasing along with that grin she had. She tossed her braids in an over dramatic manner and turned her back fully to him.

He slipped up behind her putting his arms about her own. He held her hands at her own waist as he laid his chin on her shoulder. "I am sure I can meet all your needs." He teased back whispering in her ear. He moaned when she shivered at his words. He turned her to him, and he moved his lips to claim hers. He did not offer a questing kiss as she had, he sought her lips with the hunger she instilled in him. It was as if the potion still lured his senses. He pulled her close, loving the feel of her solid body against his own. Her lips parted, and he teased them apart further. His tongue teasing her own till she moaned softly and surrendered against him. Feeling something shift within him, he broke the kiss. He wanted to do this right and to go farther would mean pushing matters beyond what was proper.

"I love you, Mesi." He whispered against her lips. "I have loved you for the longest time. I cannot imagine another housemate." His fingers were caught in her tangled braid as he pulled her head back to lay a lingering kiss on her lips once more. Her eyes had not yet opened.

Mesiande did not answer him for a moment as he watched her. Her face was flushed with color, and her breath was short and rapid. She swallowed hard and still did not open her eyes. "I have known for a bit." She managed to offer softly. "You do not drive the korpen very straight when I am about." She opened her eyes and smiled happily up to him.

He blushed remembering his brother correcting him for the same thing. "Y-yes, umm well I...umm like to watch you." He caught her hand and turned to head farther up the path. It would not do for Trelmar to catch them in this manner. Neither one of them were allowed to kiss Mesiande as she had not yet been to circle. A middlin was considered not of age till she had been through her first circle. Whom she chose to kiss after that was up to her but until then, he would have to be careful.

They walked back in companionable silence. Alador was deep in thought as to the events that had happened that day, and he suspected she was, as well. In less than an hour, it seemed to him as if the whole world had just changed. His thoughts seemed to tumble about, and he was struggling to make sense of them. Alador held her hand tightly till they were in sight of the first field, then stopped to look at her. "Mesi, if you could go to circle this season, would...Would you...you...ch...choose me?" He asked softly searching her face. "Or does it bother you I am not full Daezun?"

Mesiande smiled softly. She looked down at the ground, her hand running across her lips. She let the tension build as she considered his words. "It has never bothered me that you were not full Daezun." She looked up at him with mischief sparkling in her dark brown eyes. "Your eyes sparkle like a well worked metal. I would love my small ones to have such eyes. I do not put much faith in some who think that only Daezun should come from the circle. Maybe if there were more like you, it would help peace remain with the Lerdenians."

He breathed out a great sigh of relief. "So you would choose me?" He asks softly. He stared at her in amazement. He dug his fingers into his hand to see if he were truly awake.

She shook her head as she looked at him, her soft giggle emphasizing her return to her usual playful manner. "Of course I would chose you...But remember, we are to choose till the circle is finished. If a male cannot complete the ritual, one must take another." She reminded him. They both knew that the ritual was not considered complete till the first sign of false dawn. They had watched as women chose more than one male throughout the night.

"Well then, I shall just have to make sure I can complete the entire ritual." He grinned back at her. Although his words were teasing, a sense of desperation filled him. He did not want another in her furs. "I wish you were going to the circle this season." He sighed softly.

"I do too. I do not like the fact you may be chosen any more than you like that I might choose another. Do not think I have not thought so. You have slips now, and everyone knows it. Plus, I heard the adults speaking of your ritual night. The word...impressive was used." She searched his eyes as she bit her lip. "What if you do not want me after your first circle? What if you like another when you have bedded her?" Her eyes searched his with a fear he had not known she possessed.

He pulled her into his arms for reassurance as he whispered into her ear. "That, my dear Mesi, is never going to happen. You hold my heart and soul and have ever since you first popped Trelmar in the nose when he took your bow." He grinned down at her and kissed her nose gently. He chuckled as he remembered the look on Trelmar's face when she had punched him.

Mesiande laughed at the memory. "He was somewhat shocked if I recall." She hugged him to her tightly. He cheek rested against his chest as she nuzzled up under his chin. "I am so glad you are okay." She pulled away to look up at him. Her lips quivered, and her eyes were large as she whispered up to him. "At first, I thought he was going to kill you. When we got to the lake, I thought you were going to kill him. I would die if you were to be banished." She reached up to touch under his eye, which was already swelling. It was nearly closed at the moment, and he flinched slightly at the contact.

"I am not going anywhere, Mesiande. I am sorry I lost my temper so horribly. I will do what I can to contain it." He slowly pulled away from her. "I do not want to be parted from you. Although to be honest, if I was sent to another village, I would just send for you." His tone held no doubt of the choices he would make if they were forced apart.

"I need to get back before maman realizes I am not at my work." She answered looking over at the fields she was supposed to be weeding. She looked back at him and bit her lip.

"When will you go back to the mines or searching for bloodstones?" He knew she did not like field work. She loved to dig for the precious metals and stones that the ground held secret. It was like watching a small one on a treasure hunt.

"Next week we make another trip up to the dragon you found your stone at. It was large, and we only unearthed about half the dragon's bones. Potre is hoping to find a stone even half as large as yours." She worked her fingers swiftly to undo her braid so she could reset it.

"I...there is something different about that dig site, Mesi. Please be careful. I would offer to go with you, but I have my share of find and it would be unfair for me to dig further at that site." He frowned. He watched her fingers move swiftly through her hair. He did not want her to have the dreams he had. He knew they had something to do with that bloodstone or the dragon bones themselves. He had not been the same since he unearthed the stone. Dorien was right. Something had changed, and he was not certain it had solely to do with his Lerdenian blood. He knew something there had changed him, and he suspected it was more than hitting his head or gaining his magical abilities.

She finished redressing her braids before she answered him. "I am always careful on a dig. You know this." She pushed his chest playfully, once more the girl he had come to know so well.

"Yes, but this is different." He caught her hand before she could pull it back, his movement swift and certain. His grip firm. "Promise me you will be, more cautious." He insists.

Mesiande's eyes had gotten slightly larger when he had captured her hand. "I promise." She whispered, searching his face.

He did not want to let her go, but he dropped her hand and turned her toward the field. "Off with you before we are caught and both taken to task by our mothers. Being an adult has not stopped mine from nagging Tentret or Dorien." He quipped. He was an adult now, and he had his own matters to oversee.

He had a house to plan and would need to ask about a plot of land to put it upon. The compensation of land price was minimal and was used by the elders for public building improvements. One did not really own the land for the land belonged to the people, but one was allowed to build a house upon it if there were proper funds. Funds were not an issue for him at this time.

He watched Mesiande as she ran lightly back to the fields. He turned to head back to the village. He had not gone far and when he glanced back. He smiled for she was already surrounded by other girls. Their eyes met across the field, and he suddenly wished he was a small bug. He wondered what excuses she would give for her absence, the state of her clothing or the scratch upon her cheek.

Only once completely out of her sight did he allow himself to practically dance in a circle. He stopped abruptly as the pains of his fight with Trelmar reminded him to move carefully. He stood grinning widely. His Mesiande had said yes! They would be house mated and would raise small ones together. He could not wait the year till she was in the circle. Once she had been to the circle, she would share his bed. He planned to make sure she never wanted another in her furs. He took a few deep breaths to settle his rising passions. He would have to wait, but that did not mean it would be easy. He headed back to the village. He had much to prepare and hopefully only a year to finish it.

For the first time, Alador whistled as he walked. For the first time, he felt like he really belonged; that he was home. He smiled as he remembered how the dragon battle had ended. He laughed aloud as he headed carefully back home.

When Renamaum reached his mate lying by the shore, he noticed the dejected look as her head lay upon the ground. "Surely you are not disappointed that I killed him?" Renamaum looked a little bit offended for a moment. He glanced back at the bleeding form of the black dragon upon the ground. His lip snarled up as he thought for a moment she had wanted the black male to win.

"No." She answered sadly. Her tone was so forlorn.

When he looked back at her, he realized her gaze was so dejected that he grew very concerned. Then...what is it?" He asked somewhat in a panic. "Is something wrong with the clutch?" He circled about her and nuzzled her gently.

"No! Look!" She nodded over to where a path of acid had bathed the ground. There, in the middle of it, lay the large fish with great holes of acid eaten into it. "He ruined my dinner..."

Chapter Eleven

The day dawned bright and warm. Alador woke
with a smile and stretched upon his mattress. He winced
at the pain in his side, and the dull ache of his back was
immediately evident when he stretched. Not all the pain
was from the fight, some had been from the long night
spent in Maredeth's arms. He smiled at the thought of
that night. He had always thought there was not much
difference between being an adult and a middlin but now
he knew there was.

He touched his face. His jaw was sore, and his
nose was a bit swollen. He was fairly sure it had been
broken. He probably had at least one black eye. He could
barely see out of it, and it throbbed. He rolled up and sat
on the side of his bed. Every muscle cried out at the
effort. He stretched some more trying to work free the
aches and pains of the fight. He put on his clothes settling
for his more comfortable boots rather than the ones
given to him yesterday. It took some time for his side still
throbbed, and he wondered if he had broken a rib.
Hopefully it was just the pain of moving for the first time
since he had fallen into his bed.

He walked to the wall where a sheet of metal had
been burnished to provide a shine. He touched his face
gingerly and groaned at the swollen image that distortedly
stared back at him. He groaned at the thought of his
mother seeing him. He had managed to avoid his mother

last night, and given the day's work, she had not looked for him. Last night the circle of mourning had been held. The village had gathered together to comfort one another. There had been food and stories around a great fire remembering those that had been lost. He had hung back in the shadows not wanting to be questioned as to his condition. It had been his custom to hang back in such gatherings, and so even though his status seemed to be changing, no one called him forward or seemed concerned. The focus had been on other things. He got dressed and then glanced at his bow.

The normal routines of the village would not happen with the somber ritual that would occur to bury those that had died. It was unlikely that either Gregor or Mesiande would be practicing. None of the three had lost close kin, but despite that, it would be a sad day. You could not live in a village and not see everyone as kin. You worked together, shared circle and spent your life in the company of those in the village. Every name was known, and little escaped the gossip. They had lost six in all; two middlins and four elders. Thankfully the small ones had all been safe.

He would be required to help carry the bodies to the pyres as an adult. All six would be carried and sent to the gods at the same time. His body protested at that thought, and he groaned out softly. He forced himself to lean against the wall and stretch his feet back one at a time. He had to loosen up.

He could not remember a time when they had sent so many to the gods at the same time. He had not personally chosen a god to follow and so was still open to all the paths and honored them all the same. Most middlins were the same, one waited till adulthood to determine a path. It was said that a god chose the Daezun and not the other way around. He did not see how this could be as he had never seen any sign that the gods existed. The dragons existed, and the tale was that the gods had made them, but this was a matter of faith. He was fairly sure if the gods were real than they were not nice. Alador remembered when he had prayed as a small one for help with Trelmar and had never seen a single sign. In fact, things had gotten worse over time, not better. He had prayed to Kronos to bring fire and consume Trelmar. It was too bad it had not been Trelmar consumed by the fire of the dragon. That was a loss he would not have mourned.

Alador sighed as he headed for the door. He took a deep breath and forced himself through it. He might as well get it over with. His mother was going to see him eventually. He could smell the fresh bread rising up from the kitchen below his room. He stepped outside and looked about. The marks of the dragon were still visible from the top of the stairs that led to the bedrooms above. Blackened walls and rooftops marked the path of the dragon's breath. Slowly he descended the steps. The typical morning bustle of the village was absent, and the strange silence was eerie even knowing its cause.

Alador stepped into the kitchen. Tentret glanced up at his brother and gave a slight nod, not really noticing Alador as he dug into a bowl of porridge and a large portion of steaming bread. His mother had her back to him as he slipped into his seat at the table. He grabbed a bowl and filled it from the pot at the center of the table. He was trying to keep his head down. As his mother was bustling about, she slipped a mug of steaming korpen milk and a large piece of buttered bread onto the table next to him. He breathed a sigh of relief that mornings were so routine that no one really paid much attention.

His relief was shattered when his little sister, Sofie, suddenly bounced into the room.

"Korpen dung! Alador, what happened to your face?" Sofie's eyes were large as she stared at her brother's battered face.

He groaned inwardly as his mother spun about to look at him. She stalked over and tipped his face up. "Fighting again? You have only been an adult for a day, and you have already been fighting?" She tsked loudly as she moved his chin first right then left.

Alador winced as the pain shot through his face at the rough movements. He did not meet her eyes for he knew he was not supposed to lay a finger on a middlin. He did not want to admit he had already broken laws when he had only been an adult a few hours. "I am fine, Maman." He uttered dejectedly.

His manner was not lost on Tentret. "He is a middlin, Alador. You cannot touch him any longer. If you have a complaint, you will need to speak to an elder or his mother." Tentret rose up from the table and moved his dishes to the sideboard for Sofie to clean later.

"Oh! You fought Trelmar, again?" Sofie clapped her hands over her mouth realizing that this could get Alador into serious trouble now that he was an adult.

Alador's mother had not let go of his chin to both his dismay and discomfort. "Well...if you did touch him, I hope it was worth your while and that he looks worse than you do." She finally let him go as she eyed him, a strange mischievous grin replacing the harsh scrutiny she had carried only moments before. "Sofie, isn't it sad that Alador is so accident prone? I mean last night, he fell right down them stairs to his bedroom. It is outright surprising that he didn't just wake everyone right up."

Tentret scoffed in disgust and strode from the room. Sofie looked at her mother in confusion, but when she saw her mother's pointed and mischievous gaze, seemed to get the point. "Oh yes, Maman. I shall forever be teasing him about not being able to hold his ale now that he is an adult. Why, I saw just this morning that Alador was putting a new rail handle along the wall." Sophie grinned at Alador, her expression was sly and calculating.

Alador groaned for his sister had been begging for a handrail to the upstairs for a year now, and the rest of them saw no need. It was his sister that was forever fearing falling down those stairs. He knew without asking that this tale was going to require him to put up that rail she had been wanting so badly. "I will start working on it as soon as I eat." His voice held the exasperation he felt. His body ached, and he truthfully didn't feel like moving at all.

His mother chuckled as she went back to the rest of the day's baking. Most of the cooking this time of the year was done in the morning as the late afternoons would soon begin to be too hot for the kitchen fires to be burning. Alador glared at Sofie, but she just giggled and bounced from the room as was her manner. That was not how he had wanted to spend his morning, and this afternoon would be given to the village. He had been hoping to search out Mesiande and help her with whatever task she had been set to.

Once he was finished eating, Alador put the dishes on the sideboard along with the pot of porridge. He then headed out and around the house to look for odds and ends of wood that would make a hand rail. It didn't' take him long to sort out some thinner tree tops and saplings to work with. Soon he was on the stairs putting up a proper rail, all the while fuming at the fact that he would have to allow others to think it was for his benefit. It was his own fault for needing a story to explain his face, but surely his mother could have come up with something more manly. The truth was, the two of them probably had planned this for the next time he fought so Sofie could have her railing. Alador huffed in disgust of that possible conspiracy.

"Odd day to fix yar steps." Gregor's light hearted tone held the warmth and life that endeared him to Alador.

Alador nodded, not turning to look at his friend. "Umm yes. Sofie has been after me forever to put this up. With no duties assigned. I thought I would see to it." He managed to say pounding in another nail. He turned to look at his friend.

"By the gods, Alador, for her or for yah?" Gregor peered at his friend's battered face. He searched Alador's face with a surprised look. He staggered back putting his hands over his eyes. "Spare me, Krona." He mocked as if he needed protected by the gods, so gruesome was the sight of Alador's face.

"Well the story is...for me." Alador sat down on the steps rather dejected. He looked up at Gregor. His point more than clear.

"What was it this time?" Gregor moved to sit the step below him, angled so he could see his friend. "Yah look like a korpen stepped on yar face." His teasing settling somewhat although he was still not quite looking at Alador and his hand up as if hiding his eyes.

"He tried to kiss Mesi." Alador admitted. He looked at his friend. "I know she probably could have handled it, but I just got so angry. I nearly killed him,

Gregor." He looked down at his worn boots. He rubbed the back of his hand absently.

Gregor looked at him in disbelief. "And Mesi didn't kill him herself?

Alador looked down at his own bruised knuckles with a sheepish grin. "I didn't exactly give her time.

"No one would miss him." Gregor spat out. "I wonder what story his mother will tell. He dare not say he was fighting yah for it might come out as to why. He knows he can't be kissing on middlins, especially ones not wanting to be kissed. While yah would be in trouble, it is clear he would be, as well. I think this is one incident that no one will want brought to the light of day." Gregor looked up at him, his gaze reassuring.

Alador looked at him and nodded. "I am lucky, in that, I was not the one to draw a knife. And once Trelmar was in trouble, I am sure many would come forward." Both men sat quietly for a bit.

Gregor suddenly grinned. "So yah fell down the stairs, I am going to have so much fun with this one."

Alador attempted to push him back off the stairs with his foot. Just as Gregor grabbed it and a tussle was about to ensue, Alador's mother stepped out with her hands on her hips.

"Gregor! I do not need a whole new set of stairs but, by the gods, if you break that outer rail you will be rebuilding and seeing a nice even set to go with it!" She glared at Gregor and Alador with a look that only a scolding mother could have. She turned and stomped back into the kitchen.

"How does she do that?" Murmured Gregor, his voice low enough for only Alador to hear... "We hadn't even made any noise yet."

"Sofie says she has a friend in a sprite. She has a complete tale of how this sprite watches out for maman when her back is turned. Some days…" Alador grinned at his friend. "Some days I believe her." They both laughed heartily.

"Let me help." Gregor offered. The next hour the two of them worked diligently on building the second rail against the house. Unlike many of the houses, it had not originally been designed to expand up. An indoor stair had not been built as it would have taken from vital space inside. It gave the house a misshapen appearance, but it was no more colorful in its design than any other house on the circles. When it was done, Sofie appeared and brought them both a mug of mulled prickleberry juice. Gregor made a big act out of taking the cup slowly from Sofie, and she giggled as their fingers touched.

"That. Is. My. Sister." Alador looked at his friend pointedly.

Gregor's eyes were locked with Sofie's. "Yes, and a fine sister yah have too." Gregor's eyes slowly raked over Sofie.

Alador rolled his eyes. "Off with you Sofie, Gregor is a horrid flirt and will only break your heart." He took his own mug from her as she had served Gregor first…Sofie giggled as Alador placed a hand on her shoulder and attempted to turn her towards the house.

Sofie complied but watched Gregor over her shoulder. She was so intent on watching him and grinning when he winked that she ran into the door jamb by the kitchen. She flushed with color before she ducked back into the house.

Gregor chuckled softly at the girl's response. "Hard to believe she comes from the same mother as yah."

"Cad." Alador said before taking a long drink.

"Mother hen." Gregor fired right back. "I heard she was going to the circle. She is not a small one. In fact, she has a lot of curves in the right places." Gregor's free hand mimicked Sofie's curves.

Alador snorted juice out through his nose and coughed to clear his lungs. "... My sister! Remember? And you are not due into the circle for another year." Alador reminded him, still gasping for air somewhat.

"I can wait a year." Gregor teased looking at Alador with a wicked grin. "That there would be just fine for the waiting."

Alador could feel something protective rising up. His face flushed red, and he glared at Gregor. "Stop, just...stop." He growled out.

Gregor put his hands out. One mug hand still holding his mug of mulled juice. "All right, all right." His movements intended to placate. "I mean no disrespect Al. I thought maybe to consider asking her to housemate in time."

Alador stared at him in concerned disbelief. "My sister?" He couldn't imagine his best friend and his sister like him and the elder. It just seemed, well, wrong. His nose scrunched as this picture hit him and he shook his head to free it.

"You do not think I am good enough for yar sister?" Gregor's eyes narrowed. He was usually easy going but Gregor had this thing about being good enough that would bring his temper to the surface quickly.

It was Alador's turn to placate. "No, it is not that. I just can't imagine her, well you know. With my best friend." He shuddered at the thought of Gregor and his sister doing the things that he had with Meradeth. "I am sorry Gregor. It is my sister, and you and I both know you have stolen more than a couple of kisses."

"I was just teasing Al. I would never steal a kiss from yar sister." Gregor nodded and appeared somewhat placated. "Now if she was offering..." At Alador's growl, Gregor put back out his hands. "Okay, Okay I will stop." Gregor could not help the mischief that danced in his eyes. "Oh, speaking of... yah know." Gregor suddenly grins and turns to face Alador fully. "Yah going to tell me what happened? I wanted to ask yah yesterday, but yah disappeared." Gregor paused considering. "And well, the ale was free." Gregor eyes sparkled with merriment as Alador winced at the word free and Gregor took a long drink as if to emphasize the point.

Alador sighed. He still needed to go settle that debt. He looked at Gregor for a long moment. He wanted to tell his best friend of the night he had spent. He wanted to tell him everything about the ritual. But, his brothers had protected the secret of the passageway and the contents of the ritual hut. He did not see how he could do less. Finally, he answered as he looked at Gregor with a bit of regret. "I am sorry. I cannot."

"Oh fine. Take the whole, 'I am an adult now stance.'" Gregor fired back, but his tone was teasing and he took a sip of his juice. "I will get it out of yah." Gregor promised. "Eventually."

"Any other secret...most likely. Not this one." Alador looked at his friend with certainty. Gregor needed to have the same experience he had and he had no intentions of spoiling it with his perception of the ritual. He would treasure that night forever. It had seemed almost magical in its intensity and sensation. He downed his glass and went to take Gregor's when a somber chime began to strike slowly. "We better wash up and get over there."

Gregor, distracted from grilling Alador for details by the chime, nodded. "I will meet yah there." He hurried off to change out of his field clothing.

Alador took the two mugs in and looked at his sister. She was doing the dishes and looked up to take the mugs. Her face colored when he glared at her. "Best get changed." He reminded her softly. He would talk to her another day on the subject of his best friend. He headed upstairs to change into a fresh shirt and the new boots.

The funeral was a solemn occasion. The drums pounded out a slow cadence as the six bodies were brought from where they had been prepared to where the six pyres awaited. Alador has been assigned to the second body, so had watched as the other four followed. Each body was carefully laid upon the pyre. The openings they were slid along were then filled in with branches so the fire would burn evenly. It was a warm day, and the flies buzzed about the bodies despite efforts to use herbs and liniments to repel them. It was as if life was drawn from death, and it seemed somehow fitting in the light of how they had died. The slow rhythm of the drum and the sobbing of close kin were the only sounds in the still late afternoon. It was as if even nature had stilled for the importance of the events unfolding.

Once all six bodies were properly upon the pyres, and the branches laid, one of those assigned to attend at each pyre placed sacks of incense upon the branches. It would cover some of the smell and also help the fire burn hotter. Alador had been assigned this task, and he placed eight such sacks around the pyre before him. Then, he and those who had also carried walked back out to the circle that was forming about the six pyres. The drum still beat out its slow pounding cadence. Sweat ran down Alador's neck from the effort of moving the body, and the heat. A fly bit at where the sweat pooled at his collar bone, and he swatted it absently.

As if called by the drums, family and close friends moved to each pyre one by one. They laid in amongst the branches the items that they carried. Alador watched, tearing up at the thought of so much loss. Family and close friends would lay favored possessions of the dead, or gifts for the afterlife so that when they walked with the gods, they would not do so empty handed. It had been a tradition passed down amongst the people as far back as anyone knew. Such possessions were not gained easily and so to give them up in death was a personal sacrifice to the gods as well as a honoring of the deceased. Death had not yet come close to Alador, and he was glad for it. The pain on the faces of those who mourned was palpable in the air. All the while, the drum beat slowly.

He felt something touch his arm and looked down to see Mesiande's sad face looking up at him. Her eyes glistened with tears, and she just held his arm with both her hands and looked out at the pyres. The fires would not be lit till the last item was laid and the sun rested upon the far hill. It was slowly going down. It was hot in the sun, but no one complained, the heat was easing slightly. . Although many mopped their brow with sleeve and apron, no one would leave the circle till the fires burned down slightly. He placed a hand over Mesiande's and squeezed it. There was no needs for words between them. It was a simple act of comfort. He was glad she was there.

At last the sun touched the hilltop and the last
person moved back into the circle. The flies still swarmed
and bit and the drum beat on. A brand was brought from
some other fire and one by one the incense bags were lit.
The sound of the crackling wood and the acrid smoke
mixed with the lulling smell of sweet flowers filled the air.
He watched the fire burn and squeezed Mesiande's hand
even tighter. It would kill him to lose her. It would rip the
very heart out of his chest, and he could not imagine how
he would live after. He suddenly felt very protective and
wanted to pull her close but did not dare. He did reach
down and smooth some damp hair that curled before her
eye. He gently tucked it back, and when their eyes met,
there was a slight smile.

They stood drawing comfort from one another as
the sun began to slip behind the hill. The fires raged
loudly now, and the smell of burning flesh could not be
ignored. A song began to rise, and the voices slowly
united and melded. The song coursed with the slow,
mournful beat of the drums. Alador and Mesiande joined
in. His deep tenor melding with her soft tones in a
melody that was drilled into their very hearts.

> Though Dethera walks amongst us,
> and those we love are lost.
> Let us not forget the oaths,
> for great has been the cost.

> Hamaseic holds back the storms
> that we may honor the dead.
> Reistare has blessed the crops
> that we may pass the bread.

And as the sun is lowering,
Oessyn's task is done.
They wait for Krona's blessing,
through fire each is won.

For each Dethera is waiting,
to escort onto their home.
Amongst the gods their walking,
their souls no longer to roam.

And though the people are singing,
the dragons echo in kind.
Niat is softly shining,
a calling of heart and mind.

We are the people of Dragons,
we serve the gods alone.
Through trials and battles woven,
our hearts are coming home.

We are the people of Dragons,
we serve the gods alone.
Through trials and battles woven,
our hearts are coming home.

As the song trailed off, the drums ceased. The
sound of the last note fell away slowly. As if answering to

the song, much as the great wolves that howled in the night, a strange call filled the far off hills. The dragons echoed the song with their own long, mournful calls. Although no words were spoken in that echoing cry, it was if the heart of every Daezun, living or dead, was lifted up to the gods.

Chapter Twelve

Life settled into a happy rhythm for Alador as they headed for the height of summer. Being an adult meant he had a say in when he worked and, to some extent, what tasks. He took his duty to protect the small ones very seriously. He had taken the habit of going out of the village on all trips. A small one close, to middlin age, was sent to fetch him whenever a group was going out of the safety of the circles. When he was not actively guarding, he was working on laying the foundation of the house he was building for himself and Mesiande. Unlike the usual mishmash of rooms, he had borrowed paper from Tentret and had sketched out the design he wanted. The stairs would rise from the middle of the living room to the upper floor that would contain four bedrooms. The downstairs had a cooking area with room for a long table, an area for daily living and tasks and a large bedroom for himself and Mesiande. Tentret had teased him about not being very inventive as the building was square. More than one argument had erupted in the evening over the lack of imagination in Alador's design. Dorien had just smiled at both Tentret and Alador, and said it would change over time. Houses grew just like families.

Alador was working hard to anticipate needs so this would not happen. He could imagine evenings of laughter around the table. He wanted several small ones.

He loved children. This must have been a change from his night with the elder or perhaps when he suddenly had fought the dragon for them. But since then, he found himself teaching and taking the time for the small ones he watched over. He and Meradeth would often take the youngest ones that were old enough to leave the elder's circle and take them to a small pool to play at the water's edge. He had waded in with more than one to teach them to swim.

The mating ritual was now upon them, and he already had the foundations laid. He had been using his time off of his duties to take a korpen down to the woods downriver to cut trees. A korpen could drag back two fair trees. Alador did not have the skill to make the planks for the walls, but he had the slips to see it done. He was pleased with the quality of the boards but then an abundance of slips tended to guarantee one the best efforts. Gregor had been hanging about and helping him. He had teased Alador more than once that he needed to remember his friends. So often in the evening, he would stop with Gregor at the alehouse to remember him properly, or at least how Gregor saw as proper. Gregor's help had been critical, for he knew how to set the walls and supporting poles.

Mesiande would stop by now and give suggestions to the two men. As both were working in the hot sun without their shirts, she was often joined by more than one middlin girl who was close to Mesiande's age. Then they would all leave off in a small giggling circle. Alador would have given much to know the content of those conversations as the girls were often glancing back. He got little out of Gregor during these visits as Gregor although appearing to work was more flexing his muscles and involved in antics to bring about more giggles.

When the sun would begin to set, he would often meet Mesiande down at the rapids. The noise of the water falling over the rocks would hide their voices. They would sit and talk until the darkness would begin to creep around them, then he would walk her to the boundary where they both could see the outermost circle of houses that composed the village... While he would occasionally steal a kiss, it was not as frequent as he knew Mesiande was seeking. He often found himself in positions where she had maneuvered her lips close to his. He would oblige her when there was not a chance of someone coming soon or when he felt a deep sense of control. At other times, he was afraid he would not be able to stop at mere kisses. He wanted her so badly, and her touch was more intoxicating than the strongest drink at the alehouse. He knew there were others that had not waited, but Alador wanted to do things the way they should be done. He did not want to risk returning to the state of an outcast so close when everything he wanted was just within reach.

There had been no additional signs of the red dragon. There were many theories as to why he had attacked, but no one knew for sure. The crops were all coming up well, and even the spring birth of new korpen had been relatively fruitful. Usually one or two korpen were lost each year and as far as he knew, this year none had fallen. The village as a whole was recovering from the dragon's attack. All the burned buildings were repaired, and much of the scorched ground had started a patch of regrowth or been covered with fresh dirt.

The expedition back to the bones where he had dug his own bloodstone had come with much expectation, and passed with much disappointment. While numerous jewelry size stones had been found, nothing of great value had come from the second trip. It was as if all the dragon's treasure had pooled in Alador's stone. There were grumblings that Alador should share his largess. However, the find had been truly his alone, and so no one asked.

His visions had been quiet, as well. Occasionally he would dream of a vast cave on the edge of the sea. One had to swim a short distance under water to enter it. Inside was a bed of seaweed and gleaming metals. In the center was a pool of water. Often he would picture four eggs in this nest, nestled down inside the water. He could smell the salt of the sea. The comfort as he shifted on the bed of treasure and other soft matter. He would always wake up feeling warm and happy after this dream. It sometimes was difficult to fully awaken for the vision held so much detail. He could hear the water dripping down the stalactite and onto the cave floor. It was as if he were coming home. He was glad that the cave was only accessible under water. It meant the eggs were safe. He knew that Lerdenian's often stole dragon eggs for the bloodstone mines. He couldn't explain the intensity, but he knew that it was important that the eggs were safe.

Maybe this was fueled by the one night he had dreamed that the eggs had been taken by Lerdenians. The eggs had been taken to a bloodmine. Hatched there, they were fed by their handlers and tamed as pets. This thought had awakened him one morning. He had been angry and restless the rest of the day. The dragons that were raised in these 'mines' were staked out in his vision. They were well fed but not allowed any freedom, and their great wings were regularly clipped. Once a month, they were bled near to death, and then moved. One year later, the area would be dug and the bloodstones harvested. It was cruel, and he sometimes wondered why the dragons did not unite to stop it. A full flight of dragons could release their kin. Why did they leave their fledglings to grow up in a life of such misery?

Last night, he had awakened with that dream once more. He had felt the rage of the circling dragon as he looked down at the fettered dragons. He had shared his thoughts of how they were not true dragons for they knew not the hunt or the taste of the pools of magic. This had occupied his thoughts as he worked on his house for the evening. Tomorrow was the circle, and he was trying to think of anything but being chosen. He hammered furiously trying to pound the vision of last night or the upcoming ritual far from his thoughts. He about jumped out of his skin when a voice spoke.

"I thought one had to be an adult before they could establish a home and hearth?" The lazy tone both familiar and at the same time feared.

Alador spun about to see his father. He had hoped that he would not come, and the test could then be delayed. However, his father liked to attend the circle. So far, he had been the only child of such a visit to have been brought to term and raised to naming day. It always puzzled Alador how Henrick was always chosen given he was a full Lerdenian and a traveling enchanter by trade. Yet the entire village, even the elders, oddly accepted his father.

Alador bowed low to the mage. Despite his trepidation at his father's appearance, he was still to be respected. "I was given leave to enter adulthood earlier." Alador lay down his hammer and picked up a towel to wipe his hands and face. The squared foundation and design of the lower floor house could be seen quite clearly.

Henrick's eyes followed the lines of the simple squared structure. "I see. If my memory serves me correctly, only one who is found to have skills of great value or income are found worthy for such an honor. Which has happened?" His father moved to lean back against a pile of planks eyeing his son with casual curiosity. His father was dressed in simple black leather boots and pants. His red shirt in sharp contrast seemed fitting somehow. He had not remembered his father looking quite so dashing in the past. Most mages tended to have silks or robes. There was a time when his father had worn such, but the last few visits he had moved with much more confidence and his manner of dress had been casual.

Alador smiled. "It is a rather long story. If you like, I will wash up and then we can have a drink in the inn while I explain." Alador truly enjoyed his father's visits. He was an intelligent man with a quick sense of humor. While he dreaded the testing that would occur this visit and what it might mean, he truly respected the man before him. His father had always brought him gifts, told great stories and coached him to try to bring forth the ability to touch the magic gifts that those of Lerdenian blood were oft as not attuned to learn. Up until he had found the bloodstone, he had hoped each time he could leave with his father. He had thought that surely life as a halfblooded mage would be better than a halfblooded farmer or miner.

"Yes, a drink would be quite welcome to remove the taste of dust from my mouth. I fear that the lexital seemed to insist on the dustiest of routes today." His father smiled at him, and Alador could not help but notice his father did not seem the least bit dusty. However, lexital were strange creatures that would allow a single rider, and they often found their way to dust bowls. These unique creatures had a strange curved beak with what seemed to be like the sail of a boat rising above both beak and eyes. Their neck was long and serpentine, moving side to side as they steered through the sky. Their eyes were red and rimmed in blue. Their wings were varying shades of blue with a ridge of red that seemed to arch out mid-feathers. This was especially noticeable in fight. There was a natural dip in this neck right before the body that could carry the rider. Daezun were usually too solid in stature for such a beast to be practical. Alador looked around for the lexital and smiled when he saw two middlins trying to tie it to a post, and it was not cooperating.

Alador nodded. "Let me clean up and change, and then I will join you there directly." He smiled at Henrick and then turned to put his things away. He could not help but feel his father's eyes upon him for a long moment before he heard his bright response.

"Right then, I look forward to this tale of sudden prestige"

When Alador turned around, his father was gone. He smiled and hurried home to change. His father loved a good mead and wasn't likely to turn down a chance to sit in the cool darkness of the inn. The day was definitely warm. His mother was not around to slow him with her fussing for once. He breathed a sigh of relief for if she got wind that Henrick was in the village then she would never let him go without a thousand words of questions and reminders. Or maybe she had heard and was even now cleaning up to greet him. Regardless of where she was, it allowed him to rejoin Henrick at the inn rather quickly.

His father already had a crowd about him. Elders loved it when his father came for he would tell tales of the lands and villages he visited. Perhaps it was one of the reasons he seemed not to generate the hate that most Lerdenians drew. His manner was so easy going, and he was so relaxed. He did not have the pretension of many of his kin, and Henrick's ability to tell stories seemed more along the lines of one of the elders. He would pass on gossip and news from neighboring villages. Alador suspected that the bigger reason was that Henrick would always run the tab and a free drink in Smallbrook was never turned down. Alador had learned how much coin his father must spend when he had paid the tab the day he had bought drinks for everyone.

Alador stopped for a long moment. His father was a traveling enchanter by trade. It was a meager existence though boarding and room were often free. Yet he now knew how much coin his father spent when he visited. It did not add up. He pondered this conflict of fact with a frown. How did his father have so many slips? If he had slips, why did he work as a traveling enchanter? He was unable to puzzle this out and though it occupied his thoughts, he continued on to the tavern.

Alador was welcomed with greetings by all those gathered about his father. It was much more welcoming than normal, but then they were drinking his father's slips. He often still felt himself reacting as an outsider when such attention was paid. It was getting easier on subtle matters, but such a public outcry still made him a bit self-conscious. His father's shrewd eyes were on him when he entered. They seemed to cut through the crowd to find his own gaze, and Alador shifted a bit uncomfortably. Sometimes it felt as if that gaze could see his most inner thoughts.

"Alador, lad, come join us. I have been hearing the most fanciful tales." Henrick toasted his son. "Shot a dragon did we? Ran it off?" Henrick's eyes showed just a tiny bit of disbelief. "I can barely fathom it. Did you not tell me you could barely see a second target length? Certainly getting an arrow down a dragon's maw is far more difficult. It is almost as if someone pointed that arrow for you to hear it told." Henrick's tone although jovial had a strange edge to it. He leaned forward towards Alador. "Did someone tell you where to shoot, my boy?" Henrick rubbed his neck absently as he gazed at his son.

Alador rushed to answer, somewhat flustered. He had planned to sit over an ale and explain the changes since Henrick had last come to the village. It figured someone had beat him to his father with the tale. "I...but...I-It was just a lucky shot into the creature's maw. I do not know what had stirred him up so considerably." Alador hoped his father would be deflected as the subject of dragons always seemed to draw Henrick's attention. The mage had presented himself as a bit of an expert on the topic.

"Dragons have been causing more problems as of late. They seem to be more aggressive and irritated. Maybe they are more aware of their dwindling numbers then they are given credit. After all, such admirable creatures can hardly be blind to what is occurring to their race." Henrick admitted. There was a hardening of Henrick's manner, and as if he realized it, he paused taking a drink from his tankard before continuing. "Perhaps it is part of their natural cycle. We still know little of them other than the properties of their blood."

Henrick picked up on the elders' discomfort in speaking of the bloodstone magic and changed the topic. "So, did I tell you about this ball my brother had? A

Outcast

bunch of peacocks, every one of them, bowing and scraping. Why this one man came, and I swear upon the gods, his hat was taller than a water bucket..." Alador breathed out a sigh of relief as the focus was once more off of him. He sat and laughed with the others and even helped tell a tale or two of his own. Gregor made a great showing of telling how he had to help Alador put up a rail against the house because Alador fell down the stairs, making sure to emphasize he was sober at the time. Alador took the good natured ribbing with a rolling of his eyes.

The inn soon bustled with village stories since the mage had last visited and Henrick brought gales of laughter in the way he could mimic some of the more affluent and arrogant Lerdenians. Eventually the talk turned to mining once more, and Alador's huge find that had brought in more slips than any could remember. The volume diminished as Henrick did not speak but stared at his son for far too long a moment. Alador shifted uncomfortably under his father's intense gaze.

Henrick's gaze held, and the intensity of his look remained uncomfortable. "How large was this stone?" Although his voice was soft, it sounded as if it was a loud command resonating through his body.

Despite his intentions to play down the stone, Alador found himself answering. "It was enormous. About this size." He admitted to his father. He showed with his hands the large size of the jewel. He stared at his father, concerned at how easy the truth had left his lips.

"I do not know if I have heard of one larger, Alador. You must tell me. Was it normal in its appearance? Was it cracked in some way or different?" Alador found his eyes locked with his father's, unable to look away.

He felt an urge to speak and a bit of panic as he did not want to tell him of the stone suddenly. "It was clear." He sighed with frustration at his inability to hold back the words. He was still not able to look away from his father.

"Clear?" Henrick leaned forward from where he sat to where Alador sat nearby. His eyes did not leave him. "Elders, if I could be as bold as to request, you would leave us for a time. I would speak with my son in private." The elders had not missed the exchange between the two, in fact, talk around them had died down.

Alador blinked in surprise when the elders simply nodded and picked up their tankards and wandered away in small clusters. "Is something amiss?" He asked with concern once they were at the table alone.

Henrick finally dropped his eyes from Alador. He looked about and then whispered words that Alador did not understand. A ring flared on his hand and then his gaze returned to his son. "Alador, do you know what happens when a mage takes up a bloodstone?"

Alador looked about in alarm for he could not hear anything but his father. No one seemed to be paying attention to them, but yet he could not hear them. Patrons' mouthed moved, and others were milling about as if all were normal. Alador looked back to his father and shook his head no. "I have only seen them harvested." He felt his gaze catch again in his father's eyes. He wanted to look away suddenly. His breath felt caught in his chest, and his heart began to pound. He had never felt fear when he sat with his father before, but he felt it now. Why was he suddenly so scared? That gaze held almost a predatory assessment. He knew that gaze. He had seen that look in the big marnex. They had that look right before they pounced upon a prang, their large claws ripping into tender flesh. Their fangs taking the throat in a single bite. He swallowed hard and tried to calm his breathing.

"Once the magic is drained, they are clear." Henrick whispered softly. His manner was grim and he stared at Alador as if weighing some great decision. He waited for his son to realize what he was saying, watching him intently.

Alador stared at him in confusion. His father's gaze still making him feel hunted. "You mean a mage had already emptied the stone before I found it. It is really worthless?" He shook his head in denial, grasping for any truth but the one that seemed to be looming before him. He panicked slightly at the thought of what the trader would say when he returned. His heart raced in his chest, and he wanted to run.

"No, Alador, I doubt a mage dug up the stone, drained it and put it back." Henrick grinned at his son. However, that smile did not go to his eyes. In fact, Henrick's body was tense as he rubbed his throat.

Alador sat puzzled and then his eyes flew open in alarm. "Y-You think that...that...I drained it?" He whispered. He looked about. He felt a rush of even greater panic. His hands clenched at the meaning of his father's words. Suddenly all the changes made sense. Every little thing flashed before his eyes. The water heating in the bathhouse, his sudden ability to see targets as if they were close and the dragon visions he kept having. He clenched and unclenched his hands trying to look away from his father. Trying to shove the fear coursing through him to some level he could manage.

He shook his head in denial. There had been a time when he would have gladly tested to be found with magic. It would have meant that he could have left the village and went with his father, no longer an outcast. But now, he had acceptance. Now he knew that Mesiande would accept him as a housemate. The last thing he wanted was to have to leave now. His house was already started. He had thought maybe he was coming into power. It had never occurred to him he had drained the stone.

"Did you?" The question was cold. It held an edge that made Alador quiver. Henrick slowly sat back. "Did you drain that stone, Alador? Have you finally come into your legacy, my son?" The word son held a cold contemptuous tone.

Alador wanted to run. He wanted to shout to the very ceiling that he was not a mage. "N-No!" He managed to stammer out. "I-I mean, I-I haven't s-suddenly developed any skills or... or...attributes to suggest it." Alador lied to his father for the first time.

Henrick was quiet for a long moment. Then he leaned forward once more as if some decision had been made. His manner far less predatory and Alador was finally able to break that piercing gaze. He twisted a ring on his hand and picked up his tankard. "Why are you so concerned, my son? You used to beg me to test you when I would enter the village? Now you build a house and..." Henrick paused for a moment. "Ah, it is a woman, is it not?" Henrick smiled when he realized that a woman must be involved. He watched Alador as he drank from his tankard.

The room seemed to swim before his gaze for a moment, and his stomach lurched as if he had suddenly been hit. The sounds of the room came crashing back around them. "H-Her name...well it is someone I grew up with, and we are going to be housemates when she comes of age." Alador whispered so no one else would hear. "I do not want a life without her." He felt the need to protect her from his father. He could not explain it, but the feeling was intense. "I have the means to offer a life to her now. I am more than the village half breed." Alador tapped the table with two fingers to make his point.

"Women come and go, Alador. Magic, ahhhh magic now *that* is a gift worth giving dedication." The mage sat back and sipped his tankard watching the boy. "I thought it was your dream to be the next great mage? To take your place on the tiers and show your true heritage as my son." Henrick watched him with a challenging smile.

"It is no longer mine, Father. Please, let us speak no more of this." Alador growled out the answer, his words tense. He could feel his anger and fear rising up. Alador suddenly wanted to wipe the smug grin off his father's face. He clenched his fists, once more trying to drive down the strange feelings his father was stirring up.

Henrick put his boots up on the table as he leaned back. The odd predatory manner gone, and the lazy, spoiled mage once more sat before him. "I promise you, if you do not pass the tests, I will trouble you no further." Henrick took a sip and murmured softly. "Doubtful though." Although his body and manner spoke of relaxation, the sharp gaze was not missed.

Alador knew suddenly that he would pass some portion of his father's tests. He knew that he had changed since he had found the stone. As he stared at his father, he realized his father knew it too. "I do not want to take them." He whispered hotly. "It is not the path I choose. I will make my own decisions. I do not want this. I do not want it." He was the one leaning forward now.

"I fear, my dear boy, I am not asking you." Henrick answered him in a lazy manner. He sipped on his mug watching Alador. His smile was almost mocking. "I am your father and you will be tested. If not today, then before I leave. You can suddenly shoot when before you could not see? Oh, you will indeed be tested, and you will pass." He toasted his son as if applauding his efforts.

Alador jumped up, deep-seeded fear driving him as it never had before. He finally fit in, and his father was going to take it all away. "Damned if I will." He jumped up and his chair fell back. Those closest to them were startled by the noise, and looked at the two in surprise. Henrick just sat that with that knowing smile. Alador still wanted to wipe it off his smug face. Instead, He turned on his heel and stormed out. His father's soft chuckle echoing in his ears.

He broke into a run blindly headed for the river. He moved swiftly over the fence and boundary. He found a rock out in the water at the top of the small rapids and waded out to it. He flopped down in the late afternoon sun and laid there, the sound of water rushing over rocks behind cascading over his tumultuous emotions. He had wanted to hit his father. He could never remembering wanting to hit him before. He could not remember even being upset with him before. His father had become more arrogant as he had gotten older or maybe as he had gotten older he just noticed it more.

He had never considered that he could have harvested the stone. Why had this not occurred to him? Everything continued clicking into place since he had first taken in his father's question. *Did you?* Had he drained the stone when he had pulled it free? He had taken his gloves off so he had held the stone in his bare hands. The strange dreams made sense. The dragon must have made some sort of impression or left memories somehow. The ability to see and shoot with such clarity. The boiling of the water with Trelmar. The scenes seemed to swirl about in his mind. The knowledge of where to place that arrow in the red dragon's mouth.

Alador's mind raced over the facts. Daezun did not allow those of magic to live their midst. Even healers lived on the outskirts of the village boundaries, tolerated only due to the need for such magics. The only exception to this he had ever seen was traveling enchanters like his father. But even then, they were expected to do their work, share their tales and move on. It was a solitary life, or one of traveling constantly. He imagined sharing a traveling wagon with Mesiande. The many nights spent in each other's arms between villages.

He sighed softly. She would be scorned no matter what village they entered, and he knew she would be about as welcome in a Lerdenian city as mage was in a Daezun village. It was a life that he could not ask Mesiande to live. He groaned in fear and genuine distress. Maybe his father was wrong, perhaps the stones could be drained another way. Maybe the stone was just faulty. He would rather give the slips back than risk the loss of Mesiande. Certainly that was a compromise that could be reached. Still, he had spent much of the slips on the house he was building. He had given much to his family, and it would not be fair to ask them to return it. Maybe they would, maybe they would offer to protect him from having to leave.

He had to know. He had to know how to control the magic it if it were true. He had to fail his father's test. He sat up on the rock. That was it! He had to fail the test. Certainly it was just a matter of not letting the magic appear. He thought about his father's tests in the past and what way he could best replicate it. There were two things he knew had changed. The water that had heated up in the bathhouse when Trelmar had attacked him and the ability to see a target. If that had been magic and not the spring, he should be able to recreate it. If he could recreate it, then maybe he could recognize how it felt and force that feeling away. He looked about and spotted a small pool of water protected by rocks as the water swirled past. He hopped off his rock and made his way over to the pool.

He knelt down and placed his hand in the water. Nothing happened. Perhaps he wasn't a mage, and this was just stupid. How did a mage call up their powers? He hadn't used magic words or any such thing, it had just happened. He furrowed his brow and tried to concentrate on warming the water. Again, nothing happened. This was not an option. He had to know. If his father could call forth power from him, he would have to know what it felt like. To save his dreams with Mesiande, he had to figure this out.

He took off his boots and put his feet in the pool and tried again. He growled in frustration as nothing happened. What might have he had done if he had been the one to heat the water? He sat on the side of the pool with his feet in the water and thought back to that day. What had been different when the water had heated? Maybe it was because the water was already hot? He shook his head. If he could heat already warmed water, he should be able to bring some measure of warmth to cold water. He remembered how angry he had been. He replayed the events in his head, how it had felt to see Trelmar enter the bathing hut. How angry he had been when they had pushed him under, and then how afraid that maybe they weren't going to let him back up. A sensation of tingling passed through his body as he relived the event.

He looked down at the water puzzled. Was it warmer? He sighed. Probably had just gotten used to its cool touch on his heated feet. He reached out and touched it and was surprised to discover that the water was not as cold anymore. It had gained a lukewarm feel. He slowly smiled and moved the water with his finger. He thought about Trelmar kissing Mesiande, laying his filthy hands on her, but as he did, he watched the water stirring about his finger. He was aware of a strange pull from him and then he watched as steam began to rise from the water. He smiled and kept concentrating on how it had felt to hit Trelmar. His eyes were locked on his feet and concentrated on the water before him and the idea of smashing in Trelmar's face. Soon the water boiled and steamed about his feet. He kicked at it, a little amazed that the water only felt slightly warmer to his feet.

Alador took his finger from the water and watched as it slowly ceased its frothing and bubbling. Suddenly, the sound of a twig snapped and his eyes riveted to his left. There in the brush stood Trelmar with an expression of fear and shock on his face. Their eyes met and then Trelmar slowly smiled as if some thought had occurred to him, turned and ran. The sound of crashing brush and breaking twigs resounding over the sounds of the running water.

Panic swept through Alador. How long had he been there? He knew the moment he thought it that there was only one reason Trelmar would smile like that. He was going to tell someone. He jumped up and reached for the dagger at his belt. The bully was already out of sight. Alador leaped across the rocks to give pursuit. He cleared the bank and entered the brush where Trelmar had stood. He had to stop him. He had to shut him up once and for all. He had to catch him before the middlin reached the village. He crashed into the brush at a dead run. His heart was pounding with fear as he leaped over a fallen log.

Barefooted, he stepped on a broken root sticking out of the ground. The root impaled part way into his foot, and he cursed as he hopped about trying to pull it out. He tossed the broken piece aside, not caring that he bled. The pain of the wound shot through his foot as he took a few more steps after Trelmar. The sinking realization that it was too late swept through him. He gradually came to a stop. Everything he had been trying to stop by learning to control what was within him didn't matter. When Trelmar told what he had seen, his father would know. His father had made it clear he would test Alador fully. He was going to have to leave the village. He was going to have to leave Mesiande. His hands covered his face, and he collapsed to his knees with a moan of anguish.

Chapter Thirteen

Alador slowly limped his way back to the river. He stood by the water staring at it for the longest time. The sun was setting behind the hills. The heat of the summer sun did not abate much, but the air by the river was always cooler. He slowly waded out to the rock where he had left his boots, and plopped down. As he absently washed the hole in his foot, he was desperately trying to think of a way out of the situation. He had no doubt in his mind that Trelmar would use what he had seen to get revenge. The question is, in what way? Would he hold it as a constant threat? Was he even now spreading tales of Alador's new found powers? Perhaps if Trelmar would hold it as a threat, he could bargain with the middlin. Maybe he could be bought with slips of his own. Alador grabbed this hope desperately, would greed be the only thing that could save his hopes? He sighed. He had beaten Trelmar. Somehow he did not think that he could buy his way out of this predicament. He hit the rock and then cursed, shaking his hand. He should have killed Trelmar when he had the opportunity.

He remembered why he hadn't, he hadn't wanted to leave Mesiande with that burden. Yet how would he face Mesiande now and tell her that after confessing to love her, he had to leave? What of his house he had started? He could find no answers that saved anything he had gained. He should have known. It was too good to be true. He had never truly been a Daezun and to expect that a few slips would change that was hopeless. He was going to be leaving with his father. He screamed up at the darkening sky as the sun began to set. Much to his surprise, he heard far off dragons echo back his scream. He dropped his head in dejection. It felt as if even the dragons knew his destiny.

He put back on his boots once the bleeding had stopped. He might as well face it and go back to the village. He drug his feet towards the village, limping slightly from the wound in his foot. He dejectedly climbed over the village border and wandered between the rows of crops towards the flickering lights. He entered the village as the final rays of light faded from the sky. He merely nodded at a couple of those that he passed as they waved. It was completely dark by the time he made it to his mother's home. He stopped at the door and looked at the odd little house with its thrusting additions and haphazard construction. It was so different from his own. He was planning for eventualities. His mother just grabbed ahold of life as it happened and their home reflected it. The lights of the lanterns shone out through the windows giving the house a warm and pleasant feel from the outside. The herb gardens in the window boxes were fragrant in the cooling summer air. His hand paused at the door when he heard the laughter of his family. He sighed softly for it only brought greater weight to the fact that soon his world would be crashing in around him.

He stepped through the door. The kitchen was warm still from the summer day, and the heat to him was stifling. Everything had a place, and yet it was busy. Pots hung from hooks, drying herbs by the far window were hung by their stocks. The table had been cleared from dinner, and his parents were sitting at it. His mother was hanging on Henrick's every word. Her face had softened at the appearance of the mage, and his mother was in her nicest dress. Her hair was down and shimmerd in slightly graying waves. Despite the edges of gray, in that moment she looked younger. The lantern light framed her well, and for a moment, he could see what his father found attractive in his mother. His mother always was a different person when Henrick arrived. There was a softness to her in the man's presence and her eyes were always bright and filled with joy.

His eyes met the mage's but rather than anger or disappointment, Alador saw only amusement. It was almost as if Alador running off had been just a slight embarrassing misstep. He looked at the two of them sitting so close. Had his father cast a spell upon her like he had on those in the alehouse? Did she gaze upon him like that because she loved him or because she was enthralled? Yet if it was a spell, why choose his mother? Why had Henrick chosen her? Or was it merely something that had been done after the circle had started and his mother just happened to be the one caught in his web? Henrick nodded to him and then leaned over to whisper in his maman's ear. His eyes did not leave Alador's, and Alador glared back at him. Whatever Henrick said, his mother responded by giggling like a young middlin and blushed slightly. Alador cringed for she suddenly reminded him of how Sofie had acted with Gregor.

He went over by the fireplace where Dorien sat upon the floor, playing a game of stones with Tentret. The fireplace was empty given the heat of the day, but it was still a focal point of the other half of the room.

Alador watched Tentret trap many of Dorien's stones and flip them over to claim them as his own. It was a game often played for it took skill to control the board with your own painted stones. Tentret usually won, but every once in a while, one of the other three could best him.

When Alador just stood there by the fireplace, Dorien looked up briefly and nodded to his little brother and then looked back up with concern. "Everything alright, Alador?" He asked in hush tones so as not to draw the attention of the two at the table. Tentret was so immersed in his next potential move that he did not look up.

Alador nodded and collapsed into a chair that sat back from the fireplace. He stared into its cold depths trying to work out possible solutions. His brother did not press him only watching him for a moment with a frown before turning back to his game. Tentret was clearly winning by the number of white stones upon the board. Sofie was nowhere to be seen, but then this was not new. She had a habit of slipping off with her friends in the evenings when chores were done for the day. The chair next to him sat empty. His sister's sewing lay haphazardly across the small table between them. He looked about the room. Every space of the wall was covered with things they used or needed. Only the wall above the fireplace was not filled in such a manner. There, Tentret was allowed to hang the best of his drawings. Alador smiled at one of a small one bent down by the river. She had a flower tucked into her hair, and a stick in her hand she was using to dig in the mud. He sighed softly. He wanted small ones. He wanted to father Mesiande's small ones specifically.

It had become quiet at the table, and Alador looked over. His parents were nowhere to be seen, they had slipped out quietly. He rolled his eyes. He wished his mother did not act like a silly middlin when his father was about. It was not right. Adults her age should be acting with more sense. The fact he was barely an adult himself to be making such a judgment was lost on him at the moment. His thoughts moved to Mesiande. He had wanted the same things his father wanted. He would love a chance to slip out with her under the summer stars and kiss her slowly in the moonlight. Alador shook his head realizing he was more like his father than he cared to admit. He scowled in disgust at the similarities.

A knock came at the door, and Alador jumped up in alarm. Dorien raised a brow at him but left Alador to answer it. With trepidation, he opened the door to see one of Tentret's friends. He did not know whether to be relieved or angry that it was not over with. He let him in and went back to his chair, flopping down. He did not pay attention to the laughter or the jibing that was going on between the other three men.

The charge of 'magic user' would ensure that he was asked to leave the village. He would have to leave with his father, and his only hope of return was like his father, if he came back on an enchanter's rounds. This gave him a small bit of hope. At least he could see his family and spend a few nights in the arms of Mesiande. He sighed softly. What if she moved on to another in his absence? His mother had taken others to the circle when his father had not been able to attend. He would not be welcome to stay as one who was cast out for the taint of magic. He might be able to take up work if he could learn to heal, but right now the only thing he knew how to do was boil water and a blasted fire could do that. No, the only thing to do now was to wait his fate and then leave with his father. If he wanted to be able to return, he was going to have to learn skills of use to the villages. He sighed softly in defeat. He was so lost in his thoughts that he did not notice when Dorien sat down beside him in the other chair.

"Who figured it out?" Dorien asked softly.

Startled out of his deep thoughts, Alador looked at his brother in panic and then looked about the room. He found that they were alone. He slowly eased back into his chair, his hands wringing with the depth of his anxiety.

Dorien put up a hand. "Easy little brother, they are all off doing other things. I can tell by your face that something large has happened so either your father tested you and you passed..." Dorien searched Alador's face, but Alador could not quite meet his eyes. "Or somebody else figured it out." Dorien's tone was concerned and supportive.

"Trelmar!" Alador spat out, his voice dripped with venom of his hatred.

Dorien leaned forward in alarm. His head fell into his hands for a long moment before he picked his head up slightly and looked over at Alador. "How could you be so careless? Of all the people to let know that you have come into the power that is your father's curse?" Dorien asked in disbelief.

"He was spying when I thought I-I was alone. I th-thought if I knew how to control it, I could fail my father's test." Alador defended weakly. "It-t was the only way I could think of to stay here." He ran his hands through his hair making it practically stand up. He looked at his brother with a glance begging for help. His misery was written on his face and the defeated slump of his shoulders.

Dorien sat back slowly with a deep sigh. He rubbed his face with his great hands and then looked at Alador. "I thought you always wanted to go off with your father? Why all this sudden angst about passing his test or being found out? You always used to get excited when he came into the village." He asked curiously. "You no longer have to worry about living somewhere else. You do have the funds to maintain yourself."

"That was before everything changed. I got the stone and then, everyone started talking to me. I have the slips to build a house." He paused then looked at his brother, his eyes begging him to understand. "Mesiande said she would housemate with me when she is of age. I know you have your sights set on a housemate. Would you want to never have that chance?" Alador turned his gaze back to the small one on the wall. "Never to have small ones with the one you chose to spend your life with?"

Dorien's eyes followed Alador's to the drawing up on the wall. He was silent as he considered his brother's words. "No, no I would not." Dorien admitted softly. "I am sorry brother. This is one situation I cannot help you in." Dorien sighed deeply and fell silent.

The silence in the room was heavy as both men considered the situation. "I know. I have been thinking for a couple hours, and there is no way out of it. He will tell, and I will be forced to leave. I cannot ask Mesiande to go with me, she would never be happy in a Lerdenian city, and she would be far less accepted as a full Daezun." Alador's tone suggested he was coming to a bit of acceptance though the pain was laced through his words. Alador broke his gaze from the drawing up on the wall. "Dorien, I want you to take my house." He finally whispered.

"I can't do that Alador. That is yours." Dorien protested. "There may be some other way we are not thinking of, or Trelmar may decide to keep your secret for a price. It is far too soon to be giving away your things."

"Trelmar has too much to gain to keep his silence. If he doesn't keep his silence, I won't be allowed to live in it." Alador pointed out. "I know you almost had sufficient funds to build your own. I also know you have been staying to help Maman. I will leave the plan and plenty of slips. Just promise me one thing." Alador's voice broke, and he sat and breathed deeply trying not to cry in front of his brother. Defeat was written across his body and face.

"Anything little brother." Dorien murmured softly. Dorien's tone had taken on a similar angst as he looked over at Alador with resignation and genuine distress.

"I-I will leave half the slips. I know you are going to say it is… it is too much. But…I… please take care of Mesi." A sob caught in his throat, and he had to take a couple more breaths. "M-make sure she and…And her small ones always have what you know...they...they need." Alador couldn't look at his brother any longer. "Promise me." Alador's voice cracked with emotion, and the tears he was holding back burst forth with a ragged sob.

"I swear it on my life." Dorien's voice caught slightly as he choked on his own emotion.

His brother's promise was the last that he could handle. Alador nodded and buried his face in his arms against his legs. Hunched over, he let himself cry. At one point, he remembered his brother's comforting hand on his shoulder. When his tears were finally exhausted, and his mind numb, he slowly lifted his head. He was alone now. His brother must have left him to cry it out. Miserable and out of energy for any additional thought, Alador dragged himself outside and up the stairs to bed.

The next morning, Alador rose early and headed back to the river to think. He had been restless throughout the night despite his exhaustion. It was so early that the cool morning air created fog rising off the fields as if attempting to obscure the first rays of sunlight. The birds had just begun to sing as if the world was a bright and wonderful place. He picked up a rock and chucked at a tree sending the morning song birds squawking off into the distance. He laid his bow aside and plopped down upon the bank. In frustration, he began throwing rocks into the river. The world was not a bright and wonderful place. Everything was tumbling a part, and his father would expect him to test today or tomorrow. Then there was the fact that Trelmar was out there somewhere doing something with Alador's secret.

Tonight was the mating circle so many would be preparing the tents for the center. There was food being cooked in preparation that would hold and could be left out throughout the day. The building excitement would progress as the day went on. For as long as he could remember being a middlin, he had thought about going to the circle. Now he dreaded its coming. Between Trelmar, his father's test, and Mesiande not even being ready for the circle, he didn't want to go. Why did Trelmar not just get it done and end the waiting? That was the hardest part, the waiting. He knew all the possible outcomes but not knowing which one would take place was worse than the worst of the outcomes he had predicted.

He laid back in the grass and watched the sun rise higher in the sky. He did not care about the wet dew that soaked his back. He had found comfort in water as of late. He liked the touch and feel of it. He had been to the water a lot since the beginning of summer. He let the sound of water soothe his anxiety and breathed deeply in the first warming rays of the sun. He felt like a lizard stretched out to add the warmth of the day after a cool night. Lost in the consoling murmur of the river, the gentle caress of the wind and the warmth of the sun, he fell back to sleep.

Alador awoke when the sun was much higher. Something had startled him awake, and he sat up and looked about. He could see nothing amiss, and as he glanced over at the village, no alarms were ringing nor could he see smoke or anything alarming through the trees. He rose to his feet and picked up his bow. He feathered an arrow against the string as he slowly looked about. Nothing seemed out of place, yet the feeling of something horribly wrong made his stomach heave.

Seeing nothing to cause his alarm, he slowly relaxed and put the arrow away. He decided to make his way up to where he and Mesiande often sat and talked. There was a sense of warmth and safety there. He would not have duties till after the midday bell, so he had a bit more time based on the height of the sun. He scuffed his way up river, kicking rocks that laid in his way and feeling some sense of satisfaction when they would plunk against something hard.

As Alador approached the small copse and rock they had claimed, he saw Mesiande sitting with her back to him. He was pleased to see her here. Maybe he could be the one to tell her first. Maybe she would beg to come with him, and he would not have to part with her. At least he would get one more time with her before his secret was out. He approached quietly, planning to surprise her, but noticed that she seemed to be crying. He stopped. Trelmar had beat him to it. He had told Mesiande. His heart sunk and for a selfish moment, he almost turned and fled. He found he could not. He could not leave her in such a state. "Mesi?" He called softly as he approached so as not to scare her. He moved to her side with concern and kneeled down. He reached out to push some hair from her face.

"Don't touch me." She hissed. She jerked away from him as if he repulsed her.

For a long moment, he knelt there mouth agape. Finally, he sat down beside her. He had known she would take the news of his magic hard, but he never dreamed she would reject him. She had always seemed to be okay with the presence of his father. "Talk to me. What is amiss?" He looked over at her though her hair hid her face. A small part of him almost hoped she was upset he was going to the circle or that she had fought with her maman. Anything would be better than Trelmar having been the one to tell her.

"N-nothing Alador, just...please go away." She sobbed out. Her arms were wrapped about her. Her legs were pulled up tight to her. She rocked slightly front to back.

"Mesi, what did I do?" He asked, his eyes large with surprise and concern. He had never seen her so overwrought. His heart was breaking watching her rock back and forth. "I will fix it. Just...just tell me?" His voice held begging mixed with heartbreak. He looked about protectively but saw no one else watching them.

"N-nothing. Just...just please go away." She began to sob harder. Her rocking increased with the pace of her sobbing.

"Mesi...Mesi I can't leave you like this. Please?" He reached out to pull her to him. This time, she let him pull her to him and buried her face into his chest. "Talk to me." He whispered in her ear. He smoothed her tangled hair as best he could. Her body was tense and trembling against him, and when he ran his hand down her back she seemed to freeze. He carefully put his hand back to smoothing her hair.

"I...can't." She sobbed. "I can't tell you." She shook her head against his chest. He could feel her tears soaking through his shirt.

He reached out to tip her head up to look at him. She tried to resist and pull away, but he captured her tightly to him and tipped her face up. He was surprised to see a bruise on her cheek.

"Who touched you?" He demanded. His voice held immediate rage. Her eye was already swelling, and the first signs of a black eye were forming.

Mesiande clutched at his shirt with both her hands. "Please, you can't...you can't do anything Alador. Please." She begged. Her eyes searched his with fear and pain.

Alador knew instantly by the look on her face. Trelmar had taken a path he had not considered. He had gone after Mesiande. "What did that piece of korpen dung do? Tell me!" He growled softly. His tone held no room for argument, and he still held her close to him although careful in case she had been hurt more than the bruise on her face.

"He...he said he had seen you use magic. He said he was going to tell...unless I...unless I let him..." She began to sob once more and tried to pull away in shame. Her eyes closed, and she dropped her face so he would not look at her.

"Unless you let him touch you?" Alador hissed, his eyes were hard with anger. Trelmar had taken Mesiande. He had laid his hands upon her. He had used her for revenge against Alador. This all whirled in his head as he tried to remain calm for Mesiande.

Mesiande nodded. "It hurt so badly. I did not think it would hurt. It...Everyone seems to enjoy it during the mating ritual." Her words tumbled out now that he knew a little.

Alador pushed her away and jumped to his feet. His first thought was to rip his throat out. However, when he jumped up he realized by the look on Mesiande's face and the begging posture she took at his feet that she thought he was angry at her.

Mesiande clutched at his shirt hem. "Please Alador, I-I am sorry. I did not want you sent away. I didn't know what to do. I...I, please...please do not hate me!" She begged looking up at him. "You can't do anything, or he will tell that you are a mage." Her eyes spilled over in hysterical tears and she dropped to his feet sobbing on the ground.

Rage shot through Alador has the enormity of what Trelmar had done flooded through him. He stood with clenched fists as she sobbed at his feet. Love won over his anger, and he knelt down "Shhhh it will be okay. Shhhh... I do not hate you." He tried to reassure her. "I still love you. I will always love you. I just know what I have to do now." He smoothed her hair as she lay crying. He scooped her up off the ground and headed for the village. Anger lending strength to his steps. His thoughts were a whirling mass of wanting to kill Trelmar and wanting to protect Mesiande.

"Where are we going?" She lifted her head from his chest in a panic. "What are you going to do?" Her tear stained face was streaked with dirt, and her panic was clear in both her tone and gaze.

"I am taking you to the healer's hut outside the village. You will be safe there and...I trust her to see you mended and whole. He kissed her forehead after he answered. Fueled by anger and concern, he hardly noticed her weight and his strides were steady. She nestled against him at his kiss. "I love you Mesi. I love you so much. You should never have been hurt. I am sorry." He whispered.

Her tears had given way to soft sobs and every few paces he would kiss her gently or adjust her carefully to keep her safe. She was the most precious thing in his life. How could he have not predicted that Trelmar would take his revenge out on Mesiande? He kissed her again as they approached the healer's hut.

He became concerned when he realized Mesiande wasn't answering him anymore. He moved her slightly and realized she was no longer conscious. Terrified, he hurried his pace as best he could with the girl in his arms to the healer's hut. He kicked the door frantically. "Let me in! You have to help me. Let me in!!" The healer opened the door inward without invitation he barged into her home. "You have to help her!" His voice broke with panic. He did not know what Trelmar could have done that would have made her unconscious. He knew she was upset, but something more must be wrong.

The old woman took one look at the unconscious girl and the expression of the young man that held her and nodded. "Put her on the bed." She pointed over to a hanging blanket where Alador could just see the foot rail peeking from behind it. The healer went to pull her kettle from the fire as Alador moved towards the bed.

He set Mesiande on the bed and she groaned out, her eyes fluttering open. When she realized he was letting go of her she grabbed his arm, and she wouldn't let go of him. "Please...you have to stay. You can't do anything." She begged hysterically. "Please Alador. You *can't* leave me!" Her pleas were heartbreaking, and he forced himself to sit down and hold her hand.

"I am right here Mesiande. I am right here. Shhhh." He kissed the back of her hand tenderly and pushed hair from her face. Her frantic gaze reminded him of a terrified prang faun.

She clung to him as if to let him go would be to never see him again. He watched her helplessly as she sobbed. His thumb wiping tears from her cheeks. "Shhhh Mesiande. You are safe, and I am right here."

The healer brought tea and pressed into his hand. "Get her to drink it all, it will calm her." The healer whispered this into his ear and nodded to Mesiande. The healer had not asked what had happened and seemed to know what must done. Alador met the healer's knowing gaze for a long moment and then turned to Mesiande.

"Drink this, Mesi." He moved to help her sit up. His tone was soft and gentle.

"No, you are going to leave if I fall asleep." She accused and looked at him as if to say see when he could not help but wince. He had every intention of finding Trelmar but first he had to see Mesiande safe.

He tried again to put it to her lips, but she tried to shove the mug aside. "Mesiande, Drink this!" He commanded firmly. Her eyes riveted to his in shock, but she listened to his more forceful tone.

When he did not immediately leave after a few sips, her tears had settled, so he was able to coax the rest of the tea into her. Although her hands shook and he had to help her, she managed to drink it all. He eventually sat the cup aside and held her hand with one hand and pushed the hair out of her eyes with the other. She still had tears slowly slipping down her cheeks. "I will make sure you are always taken care of Mesi, I swear it." He laid down beside her and pulled her close to him. The healer was laying a few things out on a small table by the bed and did not scold him for his laying down with her. Mesiande seemed to settle with him holding her. The healer left them, and Mesiande slowly stopped crying and then fell asleep. He laid there for another ten minutes before slipping out of the bed to go find the healer.

He realized as he approached her in the other room that he didn't even know her name. She looked up at him with a grim nod. She was an elder based on the graying hair. Her dress was a simple work smock and showed no luxuries in embroidery. Although her home was small, he looked about and realized that she had most everything one could want. Even the bed had been nice like his mothers, and the kitchen had the latest in conventions including a hand pump at the sink.

She indicated a cup of tea at the table and smiled when he looked at her worried. "Nothing in it lad but tea. I need to know what happened to your young woman."

Alador sat down and took a deep drink of the tea, finding it soothing. He carefully explained what little he knew. He actually did not know much. He knew Mesiande had said Trelmar had hurt her. He knew he had touched her before she had been to the elders for training. He knew he had found her crying and clearly in a state he had never seen.

The healer's frown of displeasure was clear, but she did not press him further. She looked at Alador for a long moment. "I will need to examine her. If you will be so kind as to wait outside."

"I promised her I would not leave." He shook his head. He looked back to where the bed lay behind the curtain. "She is scared and needs me." He pointed out.

"If this lad has hurt Mesiande as you said, I will need to examine her completely, and in ways you should not be present for." The healer's tone was gentle, and she placed a hand on his shoulder. "You need to wait outside." She commanded softly.

A strange feeling of agreement flooded over him, and Alador slowly nodded. He stood up and slipped out of the small hut with the cup of tea in hand. He began to pace as he waited. He remembered the vision of the dragon who had fought to protect his mate. He remembered how allowing such a beast to live only allowed the beast to return in anger. He had let Trelmar live and just as the dragon had stated, he had struck back in the worst way possible. The more he thought, the angrier he got. He wanted to kill Trelmar. He wanted to make sure Trelmar never hurt anyone ever again. He wanted to tell the council what Trelmar had done. Trelmar was likely counting on the fact that his secret of being a mage was worse than what he had done to Mesiande. But Alador knew his father planned to test him before the council anyway. The council would, at the least, banish him. Trelmar, well Trelmar would be hung for what he had done. He was lost in his anger, blinded from sight and sound as he smashed the cup into a post, shattering the shards in all directions.

When the healer came out, she had to call to him to get his attention. "Lad!" She hollered but wisely keeping a distance. Alador spun at the sound quickly. He searched the healer's face with real concern and anxiety, his anger abating somewhat in the face of his fears for Mesiande.

The healer put out her hands as if to show she was no threat. "She will be fine. Her fear is more from the emotions involved than the physical damage done. She has some cuts and bruises, nothing that should not heal. The physical damage appears to be minimal, but she will need to be watched for a time. She also has either hit her head or been hit. There is a growing knot on the back of her head. I think it is why she was not awake when you arrived here. In addition, given the violence of her assault, she may be distraught for a time." The healer tone was very matter of fact. "Her maman should be told. She will sleep from the tea for a time if you wish to go inform her family. It is wiser to have females about her for a time" Her look made firm the point that his worst fears had been realized. Trelmar had not just touched her, he had violated her.

Alador nodded once. He did not stop and thank the healer. He did not utter a word. He just turned and ran for the village proper. He didn't have much trouble finding Mesiande's mother, Elandel, as she was usually one of those involved in the bread making of such feasts. He weaved amongst the women towards where Mesiande's mother was laughing with a few other adult women. She stopped laughing the moment she saw Alador's face and the intent manner he had moving amongst the boards and the women.

When Alador reached her, he whispered in Elandel's ear. "Mesiande is at the mage healer's. She has been badly hurt." He placed a consoling hand on either of her arms. "She needs you." He whispered urgently. He did not mention how she was hurt. He felt it was not his place to tell her.

Elandel's concerned expression turned to one of fear and horror. She squeezed one of his hands, and when Alador let go, she turned to hurry off. Mesiande had been her only small one. She gathered up her skirts and hurried off in the direction of the mage healer's.

Alador stood for a long time. He looked around slowly at those milling about him...All around him there was laughter and the murmur of shared secrets. True joy filled the village at the coming of the biggest ritual they shared. It was a joy that Alador did not share. All his life, he had been bullied and taunted by one. Now that he was old enough to defend himself, Trelmar was now targeting those that Alador loved. The world seemed to spin about him. The noise of the village, the cascade of emotion and the smell of baking were a kaleidoscope of senses combating with what he wanted most. He stood there trembling, hands and jaw tightly clenched. A movement caught his attention and his eyes caught a familiar form entering the alehouse. His eyesight snapped the image towards him showing his nemesis laughing with his friends as he entered the doorway. Alador finally moved with purpose, but it was not just anger in his step, it was the movement of a predator.

Chapter Fourteen

Alador strode through the village with single minded purpose. His anger was so apparent that a couple of villagers stepped out of his path. He no longer cared about consequences or getting banished. He had one desire, and that was to beat Trelmar senseless. He had blackmailed Mesiande with Alador's secret. Trelmar would attempt to deflect the seriousness of what he had done with Alador's secret. There was absolutely no reason for him to stay his hand any longer. The worst that could come from beating the middlin unconscious was banishment anyway. This rationalization of what he was about to do filled his head as he crossed the ground to the alehouse. He did not even acknowledge those that waved as he approached. He entered the inn taking only a second to let his eyes adjust. Trelmar and his little band were at the bar, and his friends were about him like he was some triumphant warrior. Alador's eyes locked with Trelmar's as he turned and caught sight of Alador glaring at him by the door.

Trelmar pointed him out to his friends with a smirk. "Well if it isn't our blossoming little hero." He voice oozed with derision and arrogance.

The adults in the room looked at the bar for Trelmar's tone was one of offense and brought immediate adult attention. The bar fell silent as those about realized something was very amiss. Alador did not break stride until he was nose to nose with Trelmar. He grabbed a handful of Trelmar's shirt, his anger giving him the strength to jerk the stockier man to him. "Give me one reason why I should not kill you right here, right now." Alador hissed slowly so only those closest to them could hear. Alador could hear the scraping of chairs in the sudden silence of the alehouse.

Trelmar hid the flash of fear that had showed for a moment when Alador had grabbed him. Trelmar slowly sneered "Ahhhhh, is the little magling jealous?" He looked at his friends in amusement and then looked back at Alador with a slight pout. "Are you upset that I was first? That I was the one she squirmed beneath, crying out in pleasure?" He hissed back, his tone one of mocking. "She tasted...ever...so sweet." Trelmar licked his finger to make his point directly in Alador's face. Trelmar's friends all laughed nervously, but their eyes were moving between the two.

Alador punched him. He reared back with everything he had and punched him as hard as he could. Trelmar landed back against the bar and slid down it. Trelmar's four friends tried to jump in to contain Alador as adults in the room also rose to intervene. Trelmar rolled up holding his bleeding nose. Despite the shouts of the adults for them to stop, none of the middlins seemed to have any intentions of listening. Seeing that his friends had Alador held between them, Trelmar moved forward and punched Alador in the gut. Alador doubled up as much as the containing hands would allow. Rage filled his Alador's eyes as he growled with a feral ferocity. He launched himself at Trelmar breaking free of the hands that contained him.

Adults tried to get their hands on the two fighting men, and Trelmar's friends were shouting encouragements to the middlin and getting in the way of the adults trying to contain the situation. Alador had Trelmar with his back against the bar as the two took wild swings at one another. Trelmar was faring the worst and was clearly the one attempting to defend himself. Trelmar in an attempt to break free from the bar, launched himself at Alador, and they both landed on a table that broke beneath the force of their fall and combined weight. People were shouting at them both to stop.

Both men came up now in the center of the room. There was an audible gasp by those about as Trelmar pulled a knife from his belt and lunged at Alador. It was the gasp that warned him, but even so, Alador barely jumped back in time. The knife sliced through his shirt and left a razor of red across his midsection. Panic now filled the room for this had gone from a brawl to a life or death situation. Some adults started clearing the alehouse, and Trelmar's friends were pushed out the door. Alador was unarmed and clearly at a disadvantage. It was now his turn to back pedal. Trelmar was slicing wildly, and Alador had been forced to keep retreating. The adults were no longer trying to grab a hold of either of the men. Although, the shouts for them to stop had not diminished.

As much as he had wanted to kill Trelmar, he had intended to do it with his bare hands and so had not brought in a weapon. Trelmar lunged again, his eyes filled with hate. Alador twisted to the side, barely getting his arm from harm's way. As Trelmar passed him, Alador caught the hand and with one hand on the arm shoved down, and the hand that caught the Trelmar's hand around the knife pushed up hard and fast, the snap of the

wrist audible. Trelmar cried out in agony. Alador twisted
and jerked Trelmar to him and over his leg. Both men
tumbled to the ground the knife caught between them.
The blade sank deep into Trelmar's stomach as they hit
the ground, still half held in Trelmar's hand. Alador
twisted it, the wrist grinding in the process. Trelmar's
look of disbelief as he looked down at the knife
protruding from his stomach was met with a growl of
satisfaction by Alador. Their eyes met as Alador hissed.
"Who is laughing now?"

Alador felt a hand grab his shoulder, and he was
swung around. Before he could defend himself or even
speak, he saw a large blur. Dorien, intent on stopping
further harm, laid his own brother out cold. The big
blacksmith landed a solid punch to the side of Alador's
head. The last thing he remembered as he hit the floor
was his brother's large boot landing in the middle of his
chest. His breath left him as the room spun into darkness.

Alador's first realization was a strange buzzing in
his head. His second was that he could not move his
hands or feet. He panicked when he found that he could
not move. He tried to open his eyes, but only one would
open, the other throbbed, and he could only guess it was
swollen shut. Opening one eye, he realized he was bound
and on the floor. The buzzing turned out to be figures
talking beyond his view. The only thing in his line of sight
was a broken table. He slowly remembered what had
happened. He had landed on that table. The noises
gradually changed from buzzing, to murmurs and then
finally cleared to speech. He could hear his brother
speaking to someone beyond his view of broken wood.

Dorien sounded frustrated as he spoke adamantly. "I tell you, I spoke to Elandel, Mesiande's mother. Trelmar forced himself upon her. We all know Alador has been close to the girl since they were small ones. His outrage was understandable and may I point out that he is not the one who pulled a knife!" Dorien was hotly trying to defend Alador.

"There is a council of elders for a reason. If every villager took justice into their own hands, there would be chaos. There are laws for a reason. This is a prime example of such a purpose. This conflict was unnecessary, and Trelmar would have no defense when Mesiande or her family placed their accusation." Elder Velkar's voice was firm and calm.

"I understand that. I am just asking that the situation be taken into consideration." Dorien pleaded. Dorien sounded frantic. He had never heard his brother sound frantic.

Alador managed to shift his head and winced for it felt as if it weighed a great deal and movement made it throb. He could see Henrick leaning against the bar arms folded. He looked amused at best. Dorien was close by, facing a half circle of elders. He really couldn't make out who all was there as his vision was still somewhat blurred. He could make out the form of Velkar, Luciesa, and Meradeth. Despite the blurring of his eyesight, the postures of the elders were not ones of amusement.

"We will bring it before the entire council. Trelmar's actions will be judged against him. The best I can offer you, Dorien, is that I will allow one elder to speak for Alador on this matter." Velkar waved a hand over to where Alador was laying. Velkar did not sound optimistic.

"Thank you, Elder. It is all that I can ask." Dorien sighed with defeat as he bowed low.

"Dorien, if Trelmar dies, there will be no mitigation." Luciesa warned. Her tone was firm and unyielding.

Dorien came up and inhaled sharply. "Mistress, please. Surely mitigation in that Alador was defending himself from a knife and what Trelmar had done to the one he held in regard?" Dorien took a step towards her pleading. "Please, I ask only that a proper hearing be held even in the event of Trelmar's death."

"First, your brother is an adult, and as such knows that he has no right of physical correction upon a middlin." Luciesa counted off her fingers. Her tone was a matter of fact and held no mercy. "Second, your brother ignored multiple commands from elder and adult alike to stop. Lastly, your brother clearly had the upper hand in this fight and could have disarmed Trelmar, but he chose to turn that knife on the middlin." She looked up at his brother and now that Alador's vision was clearer, he could tell her vote would be to see him hang.

Dorien had winced even from where Alador lay at each count upon the elder's fingers. "Yes Elder." Dorien's murmur held defeat. His head dropped as the full weight of what Alador was facing was laid out.

Meradeth placed a hand on Dorien's shoulder. "I will speak for him." She promised softly. "It is the least that I can do. I understand the passions your brother holds, and how hard it would have been to contain such fear and anger."

Alador decided that lying very still was in his best interest right now. He could not remember the last time a Daezun had been killed in anger, but he knew that his situation was perilous at best. Despite the threat of death, he was hoping that Trelmar died, then the dung of a korpen would not harm anyone ever again. His anger surged again, and he fought to contain the roaring that built up within him. He shifted slightly, and Henrick's eyes moved to him. Why did the mage look so amused? He would have expected his father to be quite disappointed in him.

"I understand, and I thank you. I can only pray to the gods that the boy lives to face his own justice." Dorien answered, Dorien's own anger edged his tone as he responded to Meradeth.

Meradeth nodded. "Take your brother home. I will check on Mesiande while the rest see to Trelmar's family." She squeezed Dorien's arm one last time before following them out.

As the elders turned and left, Dorien turned towards Alador. Alador swiftly shut his eye. Dorien moved to Alador and the big blacksmith bent over and hauled Alador up by his wrists and tossed him over his shoulder. Alador winced as he landed upon his brother's shoulder. The pain across his abdomen only second to the pounding in his head from being upside down. Alador did not fuss or even let on he was awake. He didn't want to face the elders with his head pounding as it was.

Given the bouncing he was getting on his brother's shoulder, he opened his one eye and saw the booted feet of his father. The village was unusually quiet for the day before the ritual. He could smell cooking food, but the usually bright murmur was hushed. Alador did not look left or right, not wanting to see the look on anyone's face that they may pass.

"You realize the boy is awake, don't you?" Henrick asked with an amused tone.

"Don't really care right now." Dorien growled angrily. His only sign he cared was the slight adjustment of Alador upon his shoulder.

Alador groaned. He had only seen his brother angry once, and it had not been a pleasant sight. The fact that it had been Dorien that had hit him was not lost on him. He was sure he was in for a sound beating or tongue lashing, possibly both. "Dorien, I am so sorry…" he began.

"Shut up, Alador. I really do not want to hear a word you have to say right now." Dorien's snarl of rage made Alador wince.

Alador was willing to bet on both now. He groaned in pain as his brother shifted him again. His father's soft chuckle did not nothing to improve the situation. It caught him again, why was his father so amused?

When they entered the house, Alador found himself dumped without any regard on the rug before the fireplace. He cried out in pain as his head hit the floor, the rug doing little to soften his landing. Dorien began pacing in the small living room. It was not really a very big room so actually the large man was only taking a couple steps and pivoting. His father was leaning against the door jam.

Alador slowly forced himself up with a moan of pain. "Please, untie me. I am not going to attack anyone else." He offered weakly. "I swear I will sit still and quiet."

"I can't you blasted fool." Dorien turned to glare at him, his face was red with anger. "Till we hear if Trelmar will live, you are under confinement. I hardly got permission to take you here in case this is your last day of breath so that you may spend it with your family."

Dorien voice dropped down as he said the last and then he stopped talking and just stood there staring. Alador jumped when he suddenly yelled at him. "You are an idiot! You know that? A damned idiot! The council would have seen the boy hanged. You just had to take matters into your own hands." Dorien slammed his fist into the wall leaving a very large hole. Dorien looked at the hole and then just laid his forehead upon the wall. "Great, one more thing to fix." He murmured miserably.

Alador stared at his brother. "I am sorry, Dorien. I am truly sorry." Alador managed to more moan out then say. "I never thought he would pull a knife." He should have though. He should have realized that because it had been Trelmar who had pulled the knife in the river. He groaned at his own lack of foresight.

Dorien looked between Alador and Henrick. He eventually settled his gaze back on Alador. "Tell him! Tell your father. He is the only one that can save your ass right now." Dorien knelt down. "Tell him or I will!" Dorien's demand brooked no argument in this matter. He turned Alador to face Henrick.

Henrick raised a brow. "Tell me what?" He did not move from where he leaned upon the jam between the kitchen and the parlor. His expression seemed to know despite his question.

Alador looked at Dorien with large eyes. Dorien smacked him alongside the back of his head. "Tell him now!"

"I...have...I have magic." Alador managed to croak out. The smack to the head had rocketed through his head like the ripple in a pond. His heart was pounding as he ventured a look up to his father.

Henrick finally looked interested. He uncrossed his arms and came over to the chair near Alador. He sat down and leaned forward. "Tell me Alador. What kind of magic have you found yourself possessing?" Henrick is tone was curious and yet almost as if he already knew. His eyes searched the battered young man's face.

"Well...I...can umm sight a bow from a long distance as if it were near. It is like the target jumps t-towards me." Alador answered. He searched his pounding head for what else. "And, water. I can heat up water." He answered. "I think that is it." He whispered. "Oh, and if I am in the water it does not hurt." He added the last as an afterthought. His words were slightly mumbled as the pain in his head was worse, having sat up, and then from Dorien having smacked him.

"Interesting. A blue dragon's stone then. I wonder..." Henrick sat back one arm crossed while the other tapped his chin. He stared at Alador for a long while, making Alador uncomfortable. "Do you have dreams? Dreams like you are the dragon?" He finally asked, leaning back forward once more.

Something seemed to shout through his head, causing his headache to worsen. *Do not tell him!* The voice was male, and it was commanding. His vision swam, and he moaned in pain in response. He swallowed hard suddenly nauseous. When he realized that Henrick was still waiting for an answer, he looked up.

"N-no? Why?" He eyed his father cautiously. Why did he not trust his father? Why did the voice not want him to trust his father? He corrected himself silently.

Dorien was watching them both carefully. Seeing the look on Alador's face, he went and fetched a bucket and sat it near Alador as the two men talked.

"Just something I heard once about stones so large possessing memories." Henrick answered thoughtfully. "Too bad. Now, that, would have been fascinating to explore." Henrick shrugged nonchalantly. Despite his dismissal of the question, his gaze made Alador shift again uncomfortably.

Just then both Alador and Mesiande's mothers burst through the door. A mass of maternal concern and as they glanced about, he felt like trapped prey. Alador groaned as his mother descended on him. She tipped his chin up gently and frowned when he moaned. "Well that Trelmar lad did a number on you that is for sure." She tsked softly. "We will need to clean that up and get some ointment on that."

"Actually that was me." Dorien admitted. "I had to stop him before he killed the boy. He may still have." Dorien looked at his mother with a slightly guilty expression.

"Well good!" Elandel spat out. Her hands were on her hips as she stood clearly infuriated. "I was just telling Alanis that Alador deserves a medal for beating the middlin senseless."

"Elandel, Alador is an adult now. Trelmar is a middlin." Dorien reminded her. "An adult is not permitted to lay hands on a middlin that is not his or her own child. The parent and the council are the only ones allowed to merit out justice. To violate this could mean banishment. To kill another villager usually ends in death for the accused. The council made this all very clear to me." Dorien moved to his feet.

Elandel's eyes became very large as she realized the impact of what Dorien was saying. "But he is the same age." She defended weakly. "What about what Trelmar did to Mesiande? Will that not… I mean that should count for something?" She looked at Alador and Alanis with grave concern.

"It will not matter. He has completed his ritual and Trelmar has not." Dorien sighed in frustration. It was clear he felt the same way.

Alador's eyes moved to his father as his mother let go of his chin. Henrick had remained quiet, watching Alador. He had lost that amused smile he usually carried. It was not hard to see the mage considering something intently. He sat back and ran his fingers repeatedly together. Alador shifted for his father's gaze was almost as if he was looking into his very soul.

As Alanis stood and turned to face his father, Elandel knelt down and gently kissed Alador's face on the side that was not swollen from Dorien's blow. "Mesiande is still sleeping, and the healer says she will be quite fine by tomorrow." Elandel moved and whispered in his ear. "Know this, no matter the outcome, I will always consider you a hero. As far as I am concerned, you are my son." She stood up as Alador just nodded once too choked up to respond. Elandel's eyes filled with tears in response to the emotion in Alador's face. She managed to choke out. "I need to get back in case she wakes up." She turned to leave the room.

"Elandel..." Alador called softly, finding his voice. Mesiande's mother turned to look down where he sat upon the floor. Alador swallowed hard and hoarsely begged. "Please do not tell her if she wakes up. Wait till she is on her feet and able to understand." The pain in his voice was apparent to everyone in the room. His one open eye met hers pleading. Mesiande's mother blinked back the resurgence of tears and nodded once. She hurried from the home, a soft sob heard as she went out the door.

As soon as the door closed, Alanis turned to Henrick. "Can you not do anything?" She pleaded desperately. She sank to Henrick's feet by the chair and grabbed a hold of the mage's hand. Her voice was softly begging. "I do not want to see him executed. I always thought he would go with you one day. I would rather he was far away than with the gods. Henrick, please, I beg you." Alanis put her face into Henrick's hand.

Henrick looked between them. There was a silence as they all looked at the mage. For a second, Alador thought he saw something in his father's eyes that indicated he had no intentions of helping. The glance was almost feral and triumphant. It was gone as quick as Alador had seen it. Maybe with his reduced vision, he was seeing things. Henrick tipped Alanis's face up and smoothed a hair from it. "I am considering options." He finally answered softly.

Dorien flopped down in the other chair. "The council says there will be no options if Trelmar dies." Dorien's tone was one of utter defeat. "Just in case, Tentret and Sofie are readying a wagon. If he doesn't die, he will need to leave quickly. I have Tentret seeing to it that the wagon is well prepared for the long trip to the coast."

"I am...here." Alador reminded them. He would have rolled his eyes, but the first movement of them hurt. "You all speak as if I am not here. I did this, and I am more than willing to face the consequences of my choices. I have wanted Trelmar dead for a long time. I am ready to pay whatever price the council deems fit." Alador drew himself up bravely.

Dorien rolled his eyes. "Such a martyr." Dorien scoffed. "Fat lot that will do you when your head is in the noose." Dorien stood up angered once more. "Willing to pay the price, Alador? Do you not care what it will do to Sofie's chances of a house mate? What about the fact that my chosen may refuse me now? What about the fact that Mesiande will ever be known as the girl that you killed for? Martyr..." Dorien growled in growing rage and frustration as he bent over Alador. "I do not need a martyr. I need a brother." Dorien threw up his hands in frustration and went and threw himself back into the chair.

Alador could not help but bow his head in defeat. His brother had been right. He had not thought of any of those things. It had never occurred to him he was hurting anyone but himself and Trelmar. He had not considered anyone else, or even thought about how they might have felt. The sheer weight of his selfishness descended down upon him.

His mother, unsure of what to say, fell into her usual role in such situations. She hurried off to fetch water and rags and see to the blood and swelling of her son. The three men sat in awkward silence after Dorien's outburst. His father was staring into the empty fireplace. Dorien had his head back with his hand over his eyes, and Alador sat mired in his own shame.

His mother bustled back into the room. When she was upset, she cleaned. Now, she focused all that energy and angst on Alador's face. He almost wished she had left him alone for her ministrations hurt more than they seemed to help. However, when she was finished, he had to admit that he felt better. She had applied a healing cream that seemed to ease the pain. "When will Tentret and Sofie be back?" He asked finally.

"As your brother said, he sent them to gather some things." His mother said with a distracted frown. "Alador, you know we love you? I mean, I know this and that was said about you being a half Lerdenian..." She glanced apologetically at Henrick, but he was still lost in his pondering. "I...Sofie is making sure you have things a mother would send." His mother choked back tears and turned away, taking the bowl and towel away. "Besides, Sofie would just be in here wailing and weeping." She muttered as she left the room, her own soft sob barely heard as she hurried off.

Alador watched his mother's back sadly. All these years of thinking that he was unwanted. Why had he not seen the truth? Finally, he looked over at his brother. "Dorien. If I am banished, can I still communicate with you?" He looked to his brother. His eyes flipped to the mage nearby, but his father seemed to still be lost in his thoughts. His fingers were still tapping together.

"Yes. Yes, you can send in letters." Dorien answered, not uncovering his face with his hand. "In fact, you had better." He answered quietly.

"I still want you to take the house. Promise me you will still see to the things we spoke of last night." Alador's tone was quiet. His words were slow and measured.

Henrick head snapped up "You did not attack Trelmar till today. Why were you discussing being banished last night?" He gazed at Alador as if trying to see through him. Alador dropped his eyes. He remembered the alehouse and he knew that somehow, his father was able to use magic when asking questions.

"Trelmar saw me trying to cast magic." Alador admitted. "I looked up and there he was watching me. I tried to accost him then, but he ran off."

"Did you? Were you able to consciously bring it forth?" Henrick asked curiously. "Did you manage to pull even the smallest bit?" He quit tapping his fingers and leaned forward to assess his son.

"Yes, I boiled the water of a small pool. I looked up, and the bastard was standing right there spying on me." Alador's voice held his contempt. "That is the information he tried to use to buy Mesi's silence before he forced her." Alador's eye narrowed in anger once more, and a soft feral growl left his throat. His body tensed, and the ropes in his wrists made an audible sound.

"Easy brother. Your temper seems to leave a swath of damage behind your path." Dorien finally moved his hand from his face as he looked at his brother. His eyes were reddened, and he looked deflated.

Henrick smiled slowly. "Well then, at least you came into your potential before you threw away your life for a skirt." Henrick seemed to have come to some conclusion, and he smiled at his son.

Alador glared at his father. That was the one thing he did not like about the mage. He seemed to have a total disregard for women beyond the bedroom. He treated them as something to be enjoyed or explored. His manner even with Alador's mother was more like one was exploring a fine meal then a respectful regard for his mate.

Sofie burst into the room. She looked about wildly and then noticed Alador. "Oh Al. Why did you do it? You were supposed to build your house and have small ones and then Gregor and I would come live with you!" She burst into tears and threw her arms about Alador's neck as she began to wail.

Alador's mother moved to Sofie and detangled her from Alador. "Careful Sofie, he is a bit hurt." Alanis warned her daughter. "He is still tied up too." She added, pointing out the obvious. She pulled her daughter into her arms.

Sofie was sobbing against their mother and words were barely audible. "Why...tied...up?" Alanis looked over Sofie's head miserably, driving home for Alador that this was not just impacting him. He had not just hurt Trelmar.

Tentret stepped in the door. Dorien jumped to his feet as he eyed their middle brother. Alador did not hear his mother's muttered response due to the expression on Dorien's face. Tentret just shook his head no.

Alador looked between them worriedly. "What is it?" He asked in a harsh whisper. "What has happened?"

Dorien looked down at his brother, swallowing hard. He knelt and took Alador by both shoulders. "Trelmar's dead."

Chapter Fifteen

The silence was only broken by Sofie's sobbing. Dorien had stood back up and put hands into his hair as if trying to consider what to do. Tentret just stood there looking sad. Alador looked to his father. He knew in that moment that his father was his only hope of survival, but his father sat there calmly as if no great matter were soon to occur.

A commotion slowly grew outside, and Alador's eyes widened. He looked outside in the waning summer light. It would be sunset in another hour or so. He could see Trelmar's sire leading a group of angry villagers from where he sat. Certainly the village would not lynch him in his own home? He shifted uncomfortably, with his feet bound he could not even run. Fear finally coursed through him as he realized he was going to die.

His mother let go of Sofie and slowly stood up. Her eye were large and fearful. "Henrick?" Her soft, pleading whisper broke Alador's heart. The expected knock came at the door making his mother jump. Alador closed his eyes.

Dorien slowly went to the door. Alador watched him move past Tentret as if every step pained him. Alador could hear the head elder, Velkar's voice. "I am sorry Dorien. The middlin did not survive. It is time." Dorien stood for a long moment at the door. Alador

could see him fighting down his desire to strike out, to
refuse them, but then he slowly stepped aside.

Two adults stepped into the room and went to
Alador, jerking him to his feet. Alador's mother screeched
and launched herself at the man closest. "No, this is not
right. He was just... Trelmar hurt the woman he loves.
Trelmar pulled the knife! It was self-defense! Why will
you all not listen?" Her screeches of fear were shrill with
terror.

Dorien was forced to pull his own mother off and
hold both her arms behind her. Alador's eyes met
Dorien's with true regret. His mother was still screaming
outrage and obscenities that Alador had not known she
even knew existed. Tears rolled down her face as Alador's
mother fought against Dorien's grip.

Alador was pulled outside, the movement hurting
his head, into the afternoon sunlight. It was directly in his
eyes as they pulled him out the door. Most of the village
was gathered outside. Trelmar's friends were clustered
with Trelmar's family. The anger from that small portion
of the crowd was almost palpable. For all those that held
anger on their faces, he saw several with remorse.
Mesiande's friends had tears, and so did many of his
mother's friends. Alador swallowed, fear filling his heart.
They were really going to hang him. He was glad that
Mesiande was still sleeping. She would not have to see
this. A tear fell down his cheek. He swallowed hard as he
realized the actual damage that was being done today. He
was dividing a village that had been whole. He was
ripping apart his family. His brother's words of how he
was hurting his siblings echoed in his pounding head.

He was dragged past the house he was building,
and he realized all the things that were being lost this day.
He would never see Mesiande's small ones. He would

never hold her in his arms and bed. He would no longer get to see that mischievous smile when she was up to no good. It had all been too good to be true. He should have known that the gods would never allow a half breed to find such happiness. Panic finally hit, and he began to fight being pulled through the village. Despite his tied feet, he fought those that held him, panic lending strength to struggles.

The villagers followed. It was rare that anyone was hung in Smallbrook. Such violence hardly known in the tightly knit community. Alador continued to try to pull free and had to be literally carried to the tree that was to be used. Two more large adults had come forward and picked up his feet. His arms felt wrenched from the sockets as they were carrying him face down. There were murmurs of distress all about him. They finally reached the tree, the roots beneath him seemed to strangle the very ground that lay beneath them. A rope was forced about his neck, and Alador continued to squirm and fight. He could hear Sofie and his mother crying. Their piercing wails cut through his very soul, it was a sound that would echo in his ears till he drew his last breath.

He tried to pull free one last time, but the rope that tightened around his neck froze him with fear. He glanced over and saw where it was tied to a korpen. A Daezun hanging was not a quick process. The slow plodding Korpen would slowly lift him off the ground. He did not want to die this way. Surely they would give him a quick death? He was lifted to his feet, and the korpen moved just enough to hold the rope taught. He was still frozen. His heart was pounding so hard that it resounded in the headache. It was as if the death drums already pounded for him.

Velkar raised his hand for silence. The crowd fell quiet except for the sobbing of his mother and sister. Velkar turned to face Alador, looking him straight in the eye. "Alador, you willfully attacked a middlin. You forced him to defend himself with a weapon and then turned that weapon upon him."

An angry murmur went up in the crowd at the verdict. Voices shouted out: "What of Mesiande?" "That is wrong?" "Surely something else can be done." "Hang him!" Meradeth looked to Alador sadly.

Alador winced at the voices shouting out about him. The one he heard the loudest was the one calling for his death. Velkar turned and raised both hands for silence. It took a while but eventually the village calmed. "It was the decision of the full elders' circle." Velkar looked back to Alador. "Alador, son of Alanis, you are sentenced to death for the murder of Trelmar, son of Anlicie." Silence followed at the weight of the elder's verdict.

Alador moaned in response. He did not want to die. For all his bravery in the house about willing to pay for his consequences, he knew in that moment, he did not want to die. His breath caught when his father's voice broke the silence.

The firm tones of sarcasm filled the air. "I think not, Elder Velkar." His father's tone was so casual as he stepped from the crowd and stood with his hands clasped behind him.

Velkar turned back to face Henrick who was at the edge of the crowd. Everyone was now watching the two men. Henrick no longer conducted himself as the carefree visiting enchanter. He seemed taller and more imposing to even Alador. "You have no right or bearing to interfere here Henrick. You are not of Smallbrook or the Daezun." Velkar reminded him. "You do not speak for this council."

The Elder and the village turned as one to look at the mage who slowly strode to the Elder and Alador. "I claim my son by right of treaty. He is mage born and as such, as a member of the Fifth tier of the Lerdenian Empire, I have the right to claim him." Henrick was on eye level with Velkar as Velkar was higher up the hill. The two men stood somewhat close, Henrick's hands still clasped formally behind him. Alador was watching them with fear driven hope.

"Mage born? He came into power?! When did you plan to tell me of this?" Velkar demanded his voice rife with indignation. Other elders were now forming a half circle around the two men. Alador was still in the noose at Velkar's back.

A sound of outrage from Trelmar's mother could be heard nearby. It was swiftly followed by Maredeth's command to shut her mouth. Alador could not help but feel a moment of gratitude towards the elder.

"After the circle tomorrow so the boy could experience at least one season with his Daezun kin." Henrick's lazy tone held an edge of threat. "However, this turn of events has required I demand possession of him a bit early." Henrick pulled a hand around and examined his nails as if considering cutting them. He acted almost as if the whole matter was rather an inconvenience.

Velkar stared at Henrick for a long moment. Alador held his breath. He could not remember anyone ever calling upon the treaty before. Velkar nodded once. "Take him then and depart." Velkar's voice held an edge of relief. Despite this, his next words cut nearly as deeply as the calling for his death. "Alador no longer exists to this village."

Anlicie, Trelmar's mother, jumped forward. "No! No! He has to pay for what he has done. He killed my son! He needs to pay!" She tried to force her way through the elder's half circle.

Meradeth drew up and turned to place a hand on the woman's chest. "For the last time Anlicie, shut up! If Alador had not killed your son, it would be him in that noose. You would have lost your son either way. Go home!" Maredeth's command echoed firmly.

One of Anlicie's friends took her by the arm and led her sobbing away. Meradeth turned back and met Alador's terrified gaze. She gave a reassuring nod before turning her gaze back to Velkar.

Velkar turned to Alador. "You are hereby banished. The name Alador no longer exists to the people. Your name will be erased from the records." He met Alador's eyes. "Be grateful you have been mage born this day." Then as if to make his point, he slowly turned his back to Alador facing neither him nor his father.

Slowly one by one, the village turned their back to him. Many took a long moment to turn. Alador's wide eyes scanned the crowd as one by one they all turned away. Gregor was by Sofie. He turned Alador's sister away, holding her as she sobbed but not before he gave Alador a firm nod of support. His mother was one of the last to turn and even then Dorien had to turn her around. His mother sank to the ground at Dorien's feet sobbing. Dorien's eyes met Alador's and he mouthed the words 'I promise' slowly. Alador swallowed hard, his heart felt as if it were being ripped out of his chest as Dorien turned. He was alone now. He had no one but Henrick.

Henrick strode to Alador and cut him down. "Come along lad. Time for us to go." Henrick did not seem moved by the events about him. Despite that, his words were soft as he sliced the rest of Alador's bonds. Alador had never seen Henrick with a weapon so the glittering knife with its jeweled handle caught his eyes. Henrick slide the knife back into his boot and then grabbed Alador by the arm.

Alador numbly allowed Henrick to pull him through the crowd, the villagers' backs remained to him. This was worse than being banished. If he wanted to write to Dorien, it would have to be in secret. As far at the village was concerned, he was dead. His family would be required to honor that. He did not say anything as Henrick pulled him roughly into his mother's home.

"We do not have time for self-pity and regret Alador. Gather all that you want that is personal. Tentret and Sofie have already loaded a wagon for us with other supplies. If you want your chest of slips, you will need to get it now." Henrick's tone was not tender. It was not understanding. It was just commanding. "You have less than half the hour. I expect that the boy's friends and family will wish some further justice, and it is not wise for us to tarrying long enough for them to form a plan." With that said, Henrick strode from the room leaving Alador standing numbly in the center.

Alador stood, unmoving, in the center of the room. He glanced at the table. So many meals had been eaten, some with scolding and most with laughter. His eyes traveled over his mother's kitchen. She was the master of this domain, and suddenly he wished for her cooking for it really had seemed to make things better. His eyes moved to Sofie's sewing. He wondered if she and Gregor would really be housemates. Lastly, his eyes strayed to Tentret's drawings. The small one with the flower holding his gaze as tears slowly fell down his cheeks. This was home. It had always been home. He just had never realized it.

Alador did not move till the murmur of angry voices reached his ear. Henrick's words of additional justice rang in his ears. He hurried up to his room and gathered some personal items. He shoved them in a rucksack and looked about hurriedly. He did not have much. He scooped up his bow and quiver along with the sack of supplies for fletching. He ran down the stairs and to the small room in which the chest was hidden. He opened it, struggling with the lock, and removed as many slips as the ruck bag had left to carry. It took a bit to relock it as his hands were shaking so badly, and tears in his eyes made it difficult to see.

He hurried back into the central room and placed the keys upon the table. He hastily scrawled a note on the back of one of his brother's drawings leaving instructions to take care of each other with the remaining slips and to look out for Mesiande. He stood up, took one last look around. He suddenly rushed to the drawing of the small one and took it down. He rolled it up as he hurried out the door.

Henrick had the cart waiting for him. He was beckoning Alador to get in, and a crowd was forming off in the distance. Alador could see the forms of Meradeth, Velkar, Tentret, and Dorien standing between the crowd and the path to the house. Alador hopped in and turned around to watch the crowd as Henrick slapped the reins on the korpens' backs.

His eyes filled with tears once more at the chaos left in his wake. He had finally found his place. He had finally felt like he belonged. Trelmar had been right, he would never have her. The bastard had taken it all from him. He had lost his family, lost his Mesiande, his home and his village. All he knew and loved was here in this place with these people. Trelmar had found a way to torment Alador even in his death. Everything was gone! He was headed to a place where he would be truly nothing, nothing but an outcast.

ABOUT THE AUTHOR

Cheryl Matthynssens is a mother of four and a grandmother of three. She graduated from Western Washington University as an English Education Major with a minor in Psychology. She later went back and received certification as a Chemical Dependency Counselor.

Combined with a love of helping others has remained a strong passion for all things fantasy. An avid reader, rpg player, and as her family calls her, a computer nerd, Cheryl has never given up her writing or desire to share her art with others. Book two of this series, *The Blackguard,* is scheduled for release in May of 2014. In addition to these novels, she has also published two Children's Books: *How the Dragon's Got Their Colors* and *Not an Egg?!*

Cheryl also has a blog and website. You can contact her through those sites at dragonsgeas.blogspot.com or dragonsgeas.com

15817955R00146

Printed in Great Britain
by Amazon